HACKING AFFECTIONS

JANUSHI RAICHURA

To Aayushi,
Unlike the reels I send you, I hope this book does not
traumatise you.

Contents

1

Christian

———◦♡◦———

I was in the mall buying my girlfriend a bag full of clothes. I had zero fashion sense, but she was good enough at it to make it up for it.

She had already decided to buy like twenty of the outfits, but I asked her to try on another one just so I could pay for them while she was in the changing room to avoid any arguments.

She would never let me pay for her stuff. Even at dinners she would want to split the bill or pay it herself. She wasn't one of those girls who liked to show how independent she was, she just didn't think that it was fair if I was always the one who paid.

She was a little hesitant to buy the silver sequin dress, something about it being out of style, but I forced her to at least try it once.

I quickly paid for her clothes with my card, and the bill wasn't too much. Julia always preferred quantity over quality.

I bought those twenty outfits and threw in the silver sequin dress in her size as well, just in case she liked it, and waited outside the changing room with a bag in my hand.

When she walked out, she look stunning. I didn't care if it was out of style or what, but the dress made her look like a princess, especially with her dirty blonde curls running down her face.

She looked a little uncomfortable because of how tight and short the dress was, and I could see her holding her breath.

I tucked a loose curl behind her ear and whispered, "Relax, you look beautiful,"

Only then did she let go the abdomen muscles that she was holding in.

She changed back into her regular clothes and asked me where her shopping bag was.

Only then did I show her the bags filled with clothes in my hands.

"Christian, you shouldn't have!" she complained and tried to make a grab for the bags but I pulled them put of her reach and asked her if she wanted icecream.

She agreed as long as I let her pay for it and I did.

I loved buying her clothes, it was my favourite pass time activity. Whenever I wasn't typing codes in my laptop or wasn't in a meeting, I was with her.

We were going strong, and a part of me knew that she was the one. It was probably a little soon to conclude that but I liked her a lot. I liked everything about her.

But I was never sure if I loved her. That was a hard question.

We walked side by side as she liked her ice cream cone with one held and grabbed my arm with another one.

We went to buy cosmetics next and I watched as she checked out different shades against her skin.

Every now and then, she would turn to me and ask me how a certain shade looked. I, who had no experience whatsoever in buying lipsticks, would go with the good old 'it looks good,'

She bought a couple perfumes, lipsticks, and a highlighter. Because of all her purchases, she got a free makeup, which according to her was criminal to turn down.

She went through with it, and in half an hour, she was transformed from a gorgeous looking woman to an equally gorgeous looking woman.

"Christian?" she called, nervously showing her makeup.

"You look pretty," I complimented, offering her my arm. She blushed a little before taking my arm. I had asked my bodyguard to put my things in the car while she was getting her makeup done, along with the cosmetics she had purchased, so my hands were completely empty again.

Which meant that we could shop more. "Let's buy you a couple of shirts!"

I didn't argue because I had never been able to stop her from shopping for me. She ran into a shop with formal wear on display and rummaged through shirts of different shades.

She pulled out a navy blue one and I said, "I have the same one at home,"

"This has french cuffs," she replied, throwing it in the bag. She found a shade that matched my eyes and jumped in excitement.

I let put in more shirts and pants before she moved to find some coats. I had started buying entire packs in past few years but whatever she wanted to buy for me, I let her.

She urged me to try on the combinations while she looked for ties and cufflinks. Her fashion sense was extraordinary, unlike mine which didn't quite exist.

I put on one of sets she had picked out for me. I walked out, feeling a little shy as she took in my appearance. She paused for a moment before saying, "I want to kiss you so bad right now,"

I chuckled, pulling her into my arms and kissing her. She then asked me to try on a couple more suits and I did so without complaining.

After we were done, we yet again had a dozen bags and I had to call my bodyguard again to ask him to take my bags.

We were about to leave when her eyes fell on a little teddy bear holding a heart.

"You want that?" I asked her but she shook her head. I pulled her to the shop and paid for it.

She looked too shy to ask to look for more stuff, but I caught her staring at a pair of Lou Vuitton and I had to take her in.

"Christian, you don't have to-" she started, but I dragged her inside. Money couldn't buy love, but I wanted her to be happy with everything that I had.

She stared at the collection of shoes, hesitant to even try anything on.

She was young and had been working only for two years, so her salary wasn't too much, so, I wanted to buy something for her that she liked.

"Christian, I..." her voice trailed off as she looked at me with a helpless expression. I kissed her forehead softly, trying to let her know that it was fine. She tentatively pointed at a shoe and I asked a helped to help her try it.

She slipped her foot in the pair of black heels and smiled immediately.

"I think Miss Diaz has a pair that looks just like this one,"

"Oh, yes, she visited us a week ago and bought the same one." The lady informed us.

She looked up at me, waiting for me to say something, but she could see my expression change.

It had been a while since I had thought about Ruth Diaz. She was my girlfriend's boss and I had forbidden myself from thinking of her as anything else.

But then there were times like that when she crossed my mind along with a million other things about her.

I hadn't seen her since the evening at Richard's. I knew she was mad but I couldn't do anything about it. I tried texting her, I tried calling her, and she would never ignore my calls or texts. She always replied, but her tone was always too normal.

She had chosen to be someone else with me, chosen to be her true self, and I had broken her trust and I had caused her to go back to being her normal self.

I had lost her, I knew that.

A few weeks later, I realized that it was too far gone, and as much as it hurt, I had to let her go. She was happy without me, I could see that, and Dante had agreed.

I had called her a whore, had accused her indirectly of sleeping with her *brother*. There was no going back from there.

"Christian?" Julia called and I knew that she had noticed why I had zoned out.

"They suit you," I answered, offering her a small smile, but she saw right through me.

"I think I'll pass," she muttered to the saleslady before jumping to her feet.

"Pack that," I whispered to the lady before running after her as she exited the store. I asked my secretory to buy the heels in her size on call.

"Julia, stop!" I called but she didn't stop. I lightly grabbed her arm and pulled her back. "I am sorry," I spoke and she shook her head.

"Every time you hear her name, you just feel so guilty and I don't even know why!"

"I hurt her, that's why!"

She sighed and her shoulder sagged as she took a deep breath and explained, "It happened six months ago, Christian. Can you please like forget it? I can't see you so obsessed with that woman! And I can't even hate her! She's like the most patient and the calmest boss ever!"

"Well, I still feel bad and I can't do anything to change that, I am sorry,"

She sighed again but before I could say anything, my phone rang in my pocket.

It was Dante. I put it to my ear after receiving but without any greeting, he asked, "Where are you?" his voice sounded panicked and I noticed that he had made a wifi call.

"At the mall. What happened?"

"Get out of there. Fast. Get to your house, I am sending some guards."

"Why, what's wrong?"

"E.Y.E's security has been compromised. You need to get someplace safe. Take Julia with you too!" he didn't give me any further explanation, and I couldn't offer it to Julia either as I dragged her away.

We were about to reach our homes when our phones beeped with an emergency notification.

*"This is a national emergency. Citizens are requested to get someplace safe due to the possibility of an attack. This is a national emergency..."*came a robotic voice and Julia looked at me, completely freaked out.

"What is happening?"

"I am not sure either. I am just going to get you someplace safe."

The guards secured the area around my house as I got inside with Julia.

We turned on the television and watched as images and videos of the president being shot dead came up and I watched as Julia cried in horror.

I made her hot chocolate and brought her a few blankets as she sat on my couch in fear. She knew I ran a private security agency, but she had no idea about my involvement with E.Y.E.

I wasn't supposed to tell anyone, and it was history anyways. I had decided not to work for E.Y.E anymore. It was corrupted, and I could never work for such an agency.

So, I had quit after the first mission, and had thought that I would never have to face it again. But there we were, in the middle of the hall, watching as an E.Y.E official shot down the president and the people began a witchhunt for the rest of us.

"I worked for E.Y.E," I told her, taking a seat beside her. She looked up at me with her eyes wide and all I could do was stroke her cheek to bring her some sort of comfort. "It was only for one mission but now that this controversy has taken place, I think they'll take me for interrogation as well,"

"Why didn't you tell me?"

"It didn't seem that significant of a thing," I answered her honestly and she stayed quiet, slowly sipping her drink. Her eyes turned back towards the television and I told her, "Don't watch it,"

"Christian..." she muttered, her eyes widening in horror and she turned the volume on and I turned to see what had scared her.

"Among the names of the agents of E.Y.E, some very significant names have come up," on the television were

pictures of me, Ruth, and Dante.

"Ruth ma'am worked with you?!" Julia questioned but I was frozen to my spot.

And as if on cue, a knock came on the door.

Oh, God.

2

Ruth

I stared at my phone as messages started popping up one after the other. E.Y.E had made a mistake. It had unleashed Adeline.

And Adeline wasn't the kind of lady who would ever lose. She wanted revenge, revenge on Alejandro, Antsiyanah, and more importantly, she wanted revenge on E.Y.E.

They had trapped her for years, and she had bid her time, planning the downfall of everyone, and it had been a good plan.

She had manipulated a young frustrated agent into shooting the President dead, and just like that, E.Y.E's all intel had been compromised as government officials and the media had started digging.

My photo was everywhere.

The information that I had worked for E.Y.E had leaked, and I knew very well that it was Adeline's doing.

She had hated me. I never knew why, though, but she had hated me. She had hated me enough to want to ruin me.

And now, I had income tax officers, police, and all sorts of government officials running through my house and my company's buildings.

It had gotten so bad that I had to send Leah back to my mother-in-law's house.

It took me a week to sort out all the inquiries. The government had stabilized again, and the new president had dissolved the allegations on E.Y.E after no evidence was found establishing a strong connection between E.Y.E and the death of the President apart from one agent who was sentenced to death.

They would've done the same to Adeline as well, but she was smart. She had covered all the tracks and there was no proof that she even ever existed.

Just as I had put everything together in my company, I received a phone call. "Hello?" I called out tentatively, uncertain as to who the other person was.

"Reed, it's me," came Alex's voice. I sighed in relief.

"Alex, I have been waiting for you to call," I paused for a second, the grief in his voice sinking in. "What happened? Did you find her?"

"She's dead, Ruth. An is dead." Antsiyanah was my best friend at one point in life and I loved her once.

Emotions churned inside me, the news slowly sinking. I had known that she was dying, but I had done nothing. I had offered her no aid.

But it wasn't the time to blame myself. If Antsiyanah was out of the equation, then Adeline was going to crush Alex. Brutally.

I cursed before saying, "Alex, you need to run. Adeline is after you, and if she finds you, then you're dead. You better hope E. Y. E finds you first."

"I know, Reed, I know." He answered, his voice defeated.

"Where are you?"

"I would rather not say,"

I took a moment to thinking before saying, "Alex, listen to me carefully. I have a daughter too. Send Amara over here, I'll put her in an orphanage and have some nice family adopt her. You have to protect her!"

"And I will."

"No, you don't understand. If Adeline finds her, the things she'll do to her...You'd wish E. Y. E had recruited her! You need to protect her, Alex," Adeline was a horrible woman. She would torture Amara in new ways until either of them was dead.

"And I will. But I can't send her over to you. I can't risk it. You have your own daughter. If Adeline finds out you'd helped me anyhow..." he trailed off. "No, Ruth, you need to inform E. Y. E that Antsiyanah is dead. Adeline has to find out. She has to stop."

"But she won't. You know that. I'll see what I can do,"

Adeline would never stop. She hated Alejandro almost as much as she hated Antsiyanah, but more than Alex, she wanted to hurt Amara, his innocent daughter.

Adeline was a ruthless woman. She would stop at nothing to get what she wanted. Negotiating with her was of no use, but I had to try.

For the sake of my dead best friend, I had to try.

I spent the next week trying my level best to convince the senior officers of E.Y.E, but with the aftermath of the scandal shaking E.Y.E, they had an excuse to ignore me.

I was going to make them pay for it later.

Finally, I got an audience with a man named Dominic. He was Italian, or Spanish maybe, I didn't care. All I knew was that he was influential, and if I could convince him, I could convince everyone else.

He offered me a glass of scotch that I turned down as I sat in his office.

He looked at me, his black eyes piercing into mine as he sipped his drink.

"You know why I am here, Dominic,"

He did not answer immediately. He stared at me for a whole minute, perhaps only to increase the suspense, before answering, "We found him,"

If I hadn't trained myself to not react, I would've gasped, but I showed no emotions and only asked the important question, "What are you going to do to him?"

He licked his lip before saying quietly, "My sister was in Paris, in the building when it was burned,"

I knew where he was heading, and I suddenly knew that there was nothing I could do to save Alejandro.

I rose from my seat and said, "I am sorry about your sister, Dominic," before walking out of his office.

"We found his appartment," he said before I could leave and my hand froze on the doorknob. "He had already left, but we found Adelmo. And we killed him. Just thought you should know what would happen if someone were to try and protect him,"

I ignored him and the threat in his statement and walked out. He couldn't harm me as much as he wanted to. He might've been a part of the board, but I had just as much power, if not more.

I definitely had more money.

I called Alex the second I was out of the building.

"Where are you?" I questioned, skipping the introductions.

"I am getting out of here. What's going on, Ruth?"

"A senior agent gave Adeline the clearance to hunt you down and do with you whatever she pleased. She has E. Y. E's dogs with her hunting everywhere. She found your apartment and..." I trailed off.

"Tell me he's okay," I let my silence answer that question and I could feel his heart sink

"I tried to get them to back off, to talk some sense into Adeline but it won't work, A, I couldn't stop her...I am so sorry,"

"You are not obliged to do anything, Ruth. Thank you so much for your help,"

"Anytime, Alex," and with that, he ended the call. I wasn't going to give up, not at all.

So, I came in touch with the one person who could change the course of the game. Adeline.

It didn't take me long to find a way to contact her and to convince her to meet me. If I could just see her, I could easily convince her.

Alex told me it was an awful idea but I didn't care. He was my friend, one of the only people who had been there for me after my divorce. I couldn't let him die.

I knew how opposed Dante would be to that idea, so I decided to keep it from him.

Adeline asked to see me in an abandoned building but the outskirts of the city, alone. Of course, I should have never even thought of agreeing to that meeting, but there I was.

Ryan was my first love, and to be honest, the only guy I had ever loved that way. But there were times when I was so heartbroken over something Ryan had done, that I would sit with Alex and I would look at him and see everything that I wanted in Ryan.

He was a deranged murderer, agreed, but for Antsiyanah, he would do anything. He would do anything to make her smile, to keep her safe.

Ryan loved me, but that never stopped him from hurting me.

Somewhere along the road, I had developed something for Alex, but I was in love with Ryan, so he was always in the back of my head.

But I had loved him, if only platonically, and I didn't know what I would do if he were to stop existing.

And so, for his sake and mine, I agreed to drive all the way to the building alone, regretting all my life decisions the second I was out of the car.

Adeline had an armed force waiting for me, about fifteen people dressed in black and holding riffles.

Every gun was pointed at me before I had even left my car. I raised my hands in surrender as I walked out of the car, but before I could enter the building, a man gripped my arm.

"Weapons," he growled, his eyes flashing at me. I sighed and pulled out a gun from my pocket. I handed him my purse along with the gun present in my thigh holster. "Boots!"

I had no choice to pull out the knife present there and hand it to him. Only then did he let me enter the building.

He followed me inside to a man standing in the entrance of the building. The other man, this one with a surprising lack of tattoes, walked me over to a room and demanded in a firm voice, "Strip,"

I took off my jacket and handed it to him as he pulled out the weapons from it. Throwing knives were strapped around my wrists that he pulled out with no force.

He didn't seem like that bad of a man.

I took my top off and a string of knives wrapped around my waist. He didn't say a word and showed no sort of judgement for what I had done.

I took off my pants next and unhooked the knives from my thighs and a small gun hidden well.

"How were you planning to access that?" he asked jokingly as he threw my clothes to a side and handed me a single tee shirt dress.

I put it on with no complains, content that it was black in color. I had planned to use the knives there to cut the fabric from the inside and pulling out the gun and the knives but I didn't bother explain. It was unnecessary.

"I am Ruth," I spoke, only to hear his name. He stared at me for a second as if weighing my intentions before answering,

"I know. I am Cole," I smiled. Men were so easily influenced.

Cole put a hand on my back and took me to another room where they put me through a metal detector. I thought that was it, but instead of pulling me to another room, Cole took me out of the building.

A jeep was waiting for me there and Cole cuffed my hand to the back of the seat in front of me before sitting down beisde me. A woman sat on my other side and people sat behind me as well.

They took me to another location and I realized, Adeline had no intention of negotiating or letting Alejandro survive.

I had just dug my own grave.

We drove for fifteen minutes as I looked at the sky, silently feeling the cuff's size around me.

I would have to dislocate my thumb, and the pain might make me lose my dominant hand if I were to fight. I could only count on adrenaline for so much.

I counted the number of people. Six along with the driver, excluding the number of people in the jeep following us. If I were to grab Cole's gun, kill him and the woman on my right, shoot through the shackles and then take on the other people.

I pulled the gun from Cole's pocket and shot the woman to my right as Cole reached to pull out another weapon. I shot him as well, dislocating my thumb while doing so and pulling my right hand from the cuff.

There was no time to focus on the pain.

I grabbed the woman's gun, shot the man sitting beside the driver and the men behind me.

I had had more training than all of them. They were raised to be mercenaries, I was raised to be a spy.

They were trained to be strong, I was trained to be fast.

I put a gun to the driver's hand as I looked through the dead bodies for a granade as bullets started firing from the jeeps behind me. "Drive to the city. Fast."

I dialed Dante's number from the woman's phone as the jeeps started nearing us.

There was no granade, no way to take down the jeeps, I had to surrender.

Dante picked up in the first ring. "Dante, it's me, Ruth. Find me!" it was all I could say before the two jeeps surrounded us from the two sides. I raised my hands but whispered to the driver, "Drive faster,"

The driver didn't hesitate. The jeeps started speeding up as well and I muttered again, "In exactly three seconds, start driving in reverse at full speed,"

The jeeps overtook us as we drove backwards and with efficiency, the driver turned the jeeps around and sped towards the exist lane.

My heart pounded in my ear as I fixed my hand.

We were so close to getting to the city. Five more minutes. Plus, Dante was bound to track me down sooner or later.

Just as we swerved to the right we came face to face with another jeep filled with mercenaries.

"Turn around!" I commanded, but I knew it was of no use. Just as we swirled around, I saw, standing to our left in front of a jeep with her arms crossed. She raised her gun and shot the driver and I curled up instinctively and braced myself for the impact as the car swerved off the road, did a flip on the ground before colliding with a tree.

The crash was loud and painful enough to make me forget everything was a moment. I checked the phone that I had tucked safely between my stomach and legs, the only thing that could help Dante find me, and I waited as Adeline's people came to get me.

The last thing I saw before black out was a man's foot breaking the cracked window of the jeep and Adeline peeping down at me and looking like she had just won.

3

Ruth

When I came back around, I was in a bright room strapped to a chair. I groaned as I tried to adjust to the blinding light. Adeline stood in front of me with a stupid grin on her face, as if she had found a treasure, and to be honest, she had.

If E.Y.E was playing against Adeline, then I was the king. Not the queen, not a piece that a person could play with. People didn't love me. Players loved their queens, their knights, their rooks, sometimes even their bishops, but never me, yet they always had to save me. They had to treat me well, like a piece of glass, cause my survival determined their fate.

If I were to die, then E.Y.E would collapse. The media already had their eyes on E.Y.E, and with my death being linked to them, they wouldn't survive another day.

I wasn't the most powerful piece on the board, agreed, but I was damn well the most important one, and I was going to be E.Y.E's undoing.

They would have to do whatever Adeline wanted, but more than them, I was afraid for Dante. He didn't deserve to have a little sister who was always dragged into trouble.

He didn't deserve whatever Adeline had planned for him.

She splashed a bucket of water on my face, and since I was already awake, I was certain it was merely to annoy me.

"What do you want?" I grumbled, blinking the water out of my eyes. She reached out a hand towards a man on her right and he handed her a phone.

"There's media everywhere outside," she started in her usual sick voice. I tilted my head to look up at her as she started a recording, no doubt to blackmail my brother. "But they can't see what I am doing in here. That's a little unfair, isn't it? They must. No worries, I'll just show them,"

She snapped her finger and they untied me from my chair and threw me on a bed. They shackled my hands and legs and secured my neck as well as Adeline towered over me with a knife in one hand and the camera in another.

She tore the tee shirt dress open and signaled one of her men to come towards him. He appeared with a lidded plate and stood as she unlidded the plate.

A rat. There was a freaking rat on her plate. Suddenly I knew I was in deeper shit than I had earlier anticipated because I knew what she was going to do.

"I had a lot of time to read in the prison, a lot of time to imagine what I would do to you when I was to see you again," her lips curled into a cruel smile and she lifted the mouse with its tail. "I injected lithium in it. I had read about some experiments and it said that it gave them too much energy. I hope you have fun."

She dropped the mouse on my stomach and covered it with a lid and firmly secured it around the edges to make sure that it wouldn't fall off.

I mentally gulped. It was a medieval torture method. Of course, Adeline was well versed with them.

She brought a light close to the metal and I felt the rat bounce on my stomach as the heat got intense.

"The mouse will dig a hole through your abdomen and come out from your mouth,"

"What do you want?" I finally asked, putting my ego aside. She only responded with a smile before turning to a man,

"Keep applying more and more heat,"

She kept on recording from a foot away and it took the mouse two minutes to figure out that it could just escape the heat by digging into my stomach.

I tightened my grip on the shackles, my nails digging into my skin as I whimpered.

Just when Adeline thought she had had enough, she raised her hand. And slowly, the man took the rat out.

Adeline stopped the recording right after capturing my bleeding abdomen she turned back to the man.

"I have heard a lot about this..." she paused, pretending to remember the term correctly before continuing, "artificial intelligence that is on the rise. We don't want them to think we're making this up, do we?"

She took out another knife and before I could even contemplate what she was trying to do, she stabbed me. I screamed, more in surprise than in pain as I registered the pain.

The spot was right below my ribs and I could feel the edge of the knife cut my ribs as well. I squirmed as my breathing became deeper and I tried to focus on it rather than the pain. It was of no use. Luckily, it was too close to the mouse's bites and therefore, it dimmed that pain.

She wanted me to scream to satisfy herself and make my brother hurry.

"Any ideas, Larry?" she asked the man and he grinned.

"Too many of them,"

"Let's start with regular cutting, then perhaps we can resort to something more brutal,"

One of her men pulled up a chair and Adeline sat down, watching as the man made the first cut down my arm. It stung, but that sort of pain was nothing compared to what I had tolerated in the past.

She just wanted to cut me open to make the torture look bad.

"Wait!" she ordered and the man stopped immediately. "She's too comfortable here,"

That was all she needed to say for her people to unshackle me and make me stand with my wrists tied above. The man resumed his work but halfway through it, Adeline stopped him again.

"Too comfortable again. Get me some nails, a hammer, and a scarf,"

In a matter of minutes, she had those tools in her hand and I tried to step away from her as she neared me.

Larry held my left hand as she took the nail and hammered it into the wall.

I bit down my lip, not giving her the satisfaction of hearing me scream. Apparently, that seemed to leave her unsatisfied, so she raised another nail and put it through a portion under the collarbone the next time.

I screamed only to make her stop and seemed to buy it because she stopped the nailing. She took another picture and sent it to someone before leaving me there.

The position got a little uncomfortable after a while for I could not move my arms much less sit down, but Adeline made me wait for what felt like hours before she returned.

"They have offered a good price for you," she declared, clasping her hands. "But I think it can go higher,"

She mercilessly pulled out the nails and let me fall to the floor. She pulled out the knife in my stomach and forced me down on my front and I raised my neck to see her holding a whip.

My hands came protectively over my head as she began her beating, not leaving a shred of my skin over my back unharmed.

I felt dizzy as the blood poured out of my body from all my wounds and the pain started registering less and less as I started losing consciousness.

I tried to lift my head to tell her to stop but I knew it was of no use. So, instead, I used the last of my energy to make an offer.

"What are they offering you?"

"Five million dollars, clearance to leave this place, and a new identity with a visa in every country,"

"Just that much? I can double the amount,"

She scoffed in response. "I wouldn't be beating you if I wanted the money," as she raised her whip again.

"I knew where Alex is," that made her stop and she raised her head pointedly, gesturing me to continue. "You hate him more, and despite what you think, you will never be able to find him without my help,"

"I already have E.Y.E working on it,"

Now it was my turn to scoff. "E.Y.E is of no use. Alex pretended to be dead for years and they had no clue. I heard that he's returning to Spain. You'll never be able to find him once he gets there,"

The next whip was so strong that I felt it despite how sleepy I was.

"I can help you out," I managed to say. I muttered Alexander's number and Adeline called him just to see how honest I was being.

"Hello, Alexander," she spoke and shot my way a smile that told me that I was free. "If I were you, I would run,"

She threw the phone to one of her guards, a woman this time, before turning to me.

"Tell Dante we are ready for the exchange,"

A lady forced a dress over my bleeding body and the dress was black to hide the blood. It covered my arms and my neck and reached out to my ankles, only leaving my bleeding palm and unmutilated face.

The lady did something to my hair after rinsing the blood out with water and I tied them up in a bun with great difficulty cause of my cuffed hands.

A few people escorted me outside the building which was surrounded by the officials of E.Y.E and the media, and some more people who I didn't recognize.

One face stood out in the crowd, the face of Christian Walker. I tried my best to smile at him and Dante who stood beside him but I could only manage a feeble one.

The man beside me shouted, "Send the money first!"

There was no argument, no hesitation from Dante. Men appeared with suitcases no doubt filled with cash and Adeline's people rushed forward to check out their contents.

When they were satisfied, an E.Y.E official reached forward to give them a bag with new identity cards for Adeline.

They verified the authenticity all the while I tried my best not to collapse.

When they were done, a man escorted me towards Dante and I could feel the number of guns pointed towards us. Adeline boarded a chopper simultaneously and it was only after she had left with the money and the identity proofs and three of her men, that they finally let me go.

As soon as I reached Dante and Christian, the last of my will crumbled along with my strength as the adrenaline rush faded away.

"Take me away," I whispered, almost breaking down into tears.

Dante nodded and he gripped the back of my head and planted a soft kiss on my forehead. I turned to Christian, doing my best not to look weak but I knew I was only failing.

"You need to see a doctor," was all he said. He wasn't usually someone who hid his emotions. He was open and never passive about anything, but one look at his face and I could tell that something was wrong.

"No..." I choked as blood threatened to spill from my lips. Dante opened the backseat door of a car and Christian sat inside and they both helped me sit beside him.

"What do you mean?" Dante asked me softly and Christian put a soothing hand on my shoulder. I instantly melted into his touch and leaned towards him.

"Not the back..." I winced as his hand came in contact with the freshly whipped skin of my back. He nodded and kissed my temple. "Give me your phone," he didn't hesitate for even a second before handing it to me. I dialed Alex's number but just as I had expected, he had turned it off. "Can you track it?" I asked him and he nodded.

"What are you doing, Ruth?" Dante asked me.

I turned to the driver and raised my voice slightly to make it audible as I told him, "Take us to the airport," I turned back towards Dante. "Ask the doctor to meet us there. Tell her to come with her passport!"

4

Christian

It wasn't hard for me to track down Alejandro's location. I didn't ask her why, didn't choose to question her in her state.

Her dress was covering her entirely but I could see the weakness in her eyes along with mortifying pain. I watched as Dante had her drink water and offered her some drinks for her dropping sugar levels.

He offered her some food which she didn't decline and I couldn't help but stare at her completely marvelled. Ruth was a piece of art with darkness clouding herself but the way she worked made her shine through it.

She was half dead but had no complaints about anything, and no sort of regret on her face. Instead, she was willing to risk her life once again, and that too for a man who had almost killed her by accident.

"Have you found him yet?" Ruth asked in a whisper and it took me a moment to realize that she wasn't whispering, she was weak and tired and it was as loud as she could get.

"I did. He's in India," I gave her the exact location and she nodded, her eyes dropping. "Ruth, you need to lie down," I told her and she nodded.

She pressed her head against Dante who pulled her softly into his arms as she closed her eyes.

She fell asleep in a matter of moments and all I could do was watch her. I and Dante remained quiet to give her some peace.

My phone beeped and I checked unlocked it to see a message from Julia. She was asking me when I was going to be back and I had no response.

I had no answer to give her because I was blindly going wherever Ruth was. I was not leaving her after the way she had been tortured.

The driver pulled into the airport where three jets were parked. Just like everything else that she owned, they were black in color.

Dante lifted Ruth in his arms as the driver opened the door and he walked towards a certain jet with her in his arms.

I followed him wordlessly and he didn't ask me to stay back either. We walked inside the jet and I felt a sudden shift in the environment as I took in the beige interior.

Dante walked over to a lady in a white coat who instructed him to put Ruth in the small bedroom at the back of the jet.

Ruth woke up as Dante laid her down and she immediately rose to a sitting position. "It would be better if one of you was to stay here. It would help her," the doctor said.

It put the two of us in an awkward position since Dante was her brother and I would never want to see my sister naked so I knew how he felt. I wasn't dating her and even though I had no problem with being there for her, me offering it would make me sound creepy.

Luckily Dante turned to me and I knew he hated saying those words but he gripped my arm and spoke in a low and dangerous voice, "You stay and help her,"

I nodded and turned to Ruth who was, once again, looking at me like she cared for me. My heart clenched as I realized how long it had been since she'd looked at me that way and the guilt came smashing back reminding me of how I had hurt her.

Dante threw a reassuring smile Ruth's way before leaving and I knelt on her side and engulfed her hand with mine. Her hand was tiny in my palm, smaller than I had anticipated, but way softer than I had imagined.

Something took over me and I stroked the back of her palm with my fingers and pressed a kiss to it.

Her eyes looked straight into mine and I saw pain in them, lingering at the ends as I realized that it was not just physical pain that lived there.

She was hurt and broken by people, repeatedly so, and I was one of those people.

A spark passed between the two of us and at the same time, a realization slipped inside our minds. I was dating Julia.

I wasn't sure whether she pulled back first or if I dropped her hand first because of how fast it happened.

The doctor cleared her throat and I inched away from Ruth. Ruth slowly took off her dress and on any other day, perhaps I would've been enchanted, but the sight made my stomach lurch with horror.

There was blood everywhere. It was pouring out of stab wounds on her shoulder and stomach and a mysterious-looking hold on her abdomen. It flowed from her neck and her back, and I was shocked that I hadn't seen it earlier.

The doctor asked a few nurses to come in and they helped the doctor stitch up the wounds while I sat on the bed beside her, clutching her hand in mine while my other hand cupped her face.

There was something about this girl being hurt that unraveled me completely.

Every now and then, Ruth squeezed my hand when the pain got too much and each squeeze felt like it wasn't around my hand but my heart.

She had endured so much.

When the doctor was done working on her front, she had Ruth turn around and the sight was scary enough to almost make me wince in dismay.

There were whip marks all over her back, covering it completely. Her skin was almost gone, with only patches of it left in some places.

Patching up her back took a while and the pilot was scared by Ruth enough to take off without asking us to tie our seatbelts or anything.

At one point, the doctor needed to strip Ruth completely and hence, asked me to leave the room because she had surely realized that we were far from dating.

When outside, I felt like I was going to crumble. That girl had to tolerate so much and for nothing.

I knew for sure that I wasn't going to let Adeline live for what she had done.

She was going to die at my hands or Ruth's. I wasn't going to rest until I sent her to hell.

The doctor asked me to come inside the room again, and when I did, Ruth was in a pale blue gown with several tubes connected to her body.

She was lying on her front with a soft pillow underneath her stomach and upon my entry, she turned around to give me the closest thing to a smile and I took it as an invitation to sit down beside her.

I reached out to hold her hand and she didn't complain. She let her head rest and closed her eyes. We had a few more hours till we landed and I was glad that she was using them to save her energy.

"Wake me up an hour before we land," she muttered and then moved no more but her grip on my hand remained unchanged for the next few minutes after which she relaxed and eventually fell asleep.

Dante came inside the room a few minutes later only to sit and watch Ruth. He eyed my hand that was holding hers but didn't say anything, as if he knew it wasn't the time to focus on that.

I started tracking Adeline after a while and since I knew she was in the air and E.Y.E was tracking her, it wasn't hard to find her location.

She was an hour ahead of us. Even if we were to move at our fastest, she would get there before us. Hopefully, Alejandro was also on the move.

He knew better to stay at one place in his situation, but Adeline was smarter. She leaked the news of him being Mr Anonymous along with his phone, so wherever he was, he was in jeopardy and minutes away from being caught.

And if he was caught, then Adeline would know exactly where to find him.

He wouldn't survive an hour that way.

I didn't care for Alejandro. He could go to hell for all I cared, he deserved everything that came his way. But I had heard that he had a daughter who was only five and completely innocent and I was willing to kill Adeline to save the life of an innocent. Plus, he mattered to Ruth. And I happened to like her.

I woke Ruth up an hour before we were going to land and she asked me and Dante to leave her room to give her some privacy to get dressed.

When she came out, she was dressed all in black again with guns in her pocket and her hair open. She was wearing a pair of heels to war and suddenly I wasn't sure whether I admired how she stuck to her style or if I felt like she was stupid for doing so given the situation.

She had applied some lip gloss because her pale lips were shining with color and she sent a smirk my way before sitting in front of me.

"Where is she?" she asked in a voice that was so strong that no one else would've been able to tell that she was brutally tortured.

"In a motel in Gandhinagar,"

"And Alex?"

"I don't know. The number you shared with me is still off,"

Ruth held her head for a second before the seatbelt sign went on and the plane started descending.

"How long before we get to the motel?"

"An hour at least."

"I hope you have your gun,"

***

A car was waiting at the airport and I knew for a fact that Dante had called it. We got inside with two other E.Y.E officials who were waiting for us at the airport.

I gave the driver the location and Ruth buried her face in her hands as the ride started. Dante pulled her against his chest and she closed her eyes and dialed a number.

"Crey, you listen to me right now. You know how Antsiyanah always trusted me, right? Well, she left me one of her most substantial secrets, and I think that it might be of significance to you," she paused and let a smirk cover her face. "She gave me the locations of the two orphanages. Let Alex go and we'll negotiate."

She waited as Crey answered her on the other line and gave him an address before ending the call.

"I get to kill her," was she said to us and I knew that she had gotten permission to kill Adeline, and even if E.Y.E were to interfere, I would kill Adeline myself.

Adeline had stopped at a motel, perhaps to spend the night or to go out and hunt Alejandro in the middle of it. I wasn't entirely sure, so I just left it to fate.

We arrived an hour after Adeline had stopped at the motel, and Ruth was smart enough to be discreet about it.

E.Y.E agents were surrounding the hotel, but a quick call with Crey solved that and he assured us that he had sent a message to the other agents as well.

The motel was old and on any other day, I would've found it creepy. It stunk and had leaking pipes everywhere and lacked proper lighting.

It was the perfect place for a bitch like Adeline to live in.

An agent guided us upstairs to outside Adeline's room and Ruth broke the door open with a single hard shove.

With a gun in her hand and fifteen men at her tail, she marched inside, rendering Adeline speechless.

"Change of plans, Adeline,"

5
Ruth/Christian

Ruth

"Hands up," I ordered, pointing the gun at Adeline's head. All her men, who happened to be E.Y.E's spies, had a gun pointed in their direction as well, but Adeline was daring.

She knew she was going to die anyway, so she tried to casually reach inside her jacket to pull out her gun, but I shot her hands before she could get that far.

Amara flinched and only then did I notice her lying on the floor. I cursed, realizing what kind of bloodshed I had exposed a four-year-old to.

Dante quickly picked Amara up and took her outside, and only then did it dawn upon me that if she was there, then so was her father.

I turned to Alejandro and my heart clenched at his state. He was bleeding out and a significant portion of his chest was missing skin.

I gave him a look and said that Amara was going to be fine before I turned my attention back to Adeline.

I fired two more shots at Adeline's chest and let her crumble to the floor. I heard footsteps and turned to see Christian Walker and Caeser, who had taken a flight from Paris, enter along with Diana and Simon.

"Before you killed Adelmo, he had sent me the address of the orphanage. After you made the mistake of letting me go earlier this evening, I negotiated a deal with E.Y.E. They got sixty children, and trained young assassins, all in exchange for you. You wouldn't be surprised to know how quickly they were convinced to let me kill you." I could taste victory on my lips, and I savored the taste, waiting for the realization of it to sink inside Adeline's head.

"They will just detain me until they need me again, which they will, and then, you'll pay for this,"

I let my lips curl into a smile. "Oh, I don't think I will," I answered before putting the gun to Adeline's head. "Checkmate, Adeline,"

The two seconds of horror on Adeline's face were worth everything. I took them in before pulling a trigger.

And with a *bang*, it was all over.

And adrenaline came crashing down along with the pain and fatigue caused by the drugs and I collapsed into Christian's arms who held me tight against himself.

It took me a few seconds to lose consciousness, but I only gave in to the dark when I was absolutely sure of one thing: I had won. I had beaten Adeline.

Christian

I lifted Ruth off her feet as soon as she collapsed and carried her outside, away from Adeline's rotting corpse.

"Is she okay?" Dante asked me as soon as I reached him and I nodded. He was inside the car with Amara, who looked shaken to her core.

"Is dad okay?" she asked me I realized I hadn't checked on Alejandro. I wasn't even sure what they were going to do to him.

"They are just getting him to the hospital," Dante replied for me. "He'll be fine,"

Amara seemed to know him, so, I let the three of them sit in the backseat and occupied the passenger seat.

Dante sat in the middle, supporting Ruth's body and patting Amara's head every now and then.

The driver drove to a remote area on the outskirts of the city where E.Y.E had created a small safe house.

The building was in a peaceful state and very few people were inside. I and Dante took Amara and Ruth to the infirmary where they took Ruth away on a stretcher and a lady doctor made Amara sit in a small cabin.

I remained with her while Dante went to make sure that Ruth was alright.

"Hey, I am Sofia," the doctor introduced herself, giving a broad smile to calm Amara, but Amara was raised to be an assassin, she was raised to not fall for pretty smiles, so she gave no response. Sofia's smile fell, but she managed to sound just as kind and gentle as before when she asked, "Are you hurt somewhere?"

Amara looked at me as if to confirm if it was safe for her to say anything and I nodded reassuringly. Tentatively, Amara raised her tee shirt to expose her bruised stomach and I winced at how bad it looked.

Sofia's face told that she perhaps felt the same way about Amara's bruise. "Does it hurt too much?"

Amara didn't say anything for a moment and I turned concerningly towards her only to see her bottom lip tremble and a second later, she had her face buried in her hands as she violently shook.

I dropped to my knees and pulled the little girl towards me. She had been holding her tears in for so long that I felt awful for the little girl. I softly ran a hand across her back and lifted her off the floor to make her lie down on a hospital bed.

"Can you give us a minute?" I asked Sofia and she left without an argument. I let Amara cry in my arms for a while before asking, "What happened, Amara?"

Another sob escaped her lips before she managed to answer, "I miss my mother,"

I felt someone squeeze my heart. I had heard of Antsiyanah's death, but it had never crossed my mind what it would mean for this little girl.

The situation clearly demanded a feminine touch, because of the fact that she needed her mother, which I obviously couldn't provide. But I think she wanted a man's arms, perhaps all the women only managed to remind her of her grief, of what she had lost.

It took her a few minutes but she eventually calmed down and managed to put herself together if only to rub her sleepy eyes.

I immediately asked Sofia to come inside and help Amara so she could sleep as early as possible. Sofia only handed her an icepack wrapped in a thin cloth and asked her to press it over her wound for a while.

After a few minutes, I took away the icepack and asked Sofia to move Amara to the same room as Ruth so I could keep an eye on both of them.

Ruth's room was big enough for them to fit in another bed. While two men moved it in, Ruth remained motionless on her bed and it only made me more concerned.

I reached her and stroked her hair while Dante helped Amara get comfortable. I had spent the last few months denying the fact that I had some sort of feelings towards her, and I regretted it.

Perhaps I felt something for Julia, but what I felt for Ruth just felt stronger, different, it felt real, and not just some simple crush that I could ever shake off.

Ruth was a playgirl, she had a hell of an attitude and she was a bitch. But there was something about her that attracted me, something that she hid behind all the masks and hardness.

She had a soft core, and a kind heart, and I could see it no matter how hard she tried to hide it.

And that was when it struck me.

It was my freshman year of college. All of us had consumed a considerable amount of alcohol and no one was in the shape to drive.

I had bid my friends goodbye and had walked to my house all alone in the middle of the night.

My house was in a remote area because my father wished to live in peace, in solace, and away from all the nuisance.

Of course, that arrangement had its drawbacks. A mile's radius around our house was occupied by homeless people. Some, we were familiar with, the rest kept on changing.

Two men had appeared with knives and they had robbed me, and I had tried to resist them, but had ended up bleeding on the ground.

It was cold, I was injured, and I was certain that no one was looking for me.

And then, a girl came from the other end of the street.

She had a hood covering her face, and her hands were in her pockets. Her entire body was covered with navy blue matter.

She was looking around from under her hood, checking for danger, when she had found me.

Her eyes had widened and she had silently made her way towards me. It was pouring, but even with the water covering the pavement, she made no noise.

"Sir, are you okay?" she asked, kneeling beside me, her hand holding my face gently.

I groaned in response and her eyes dropped to the blood leaking from my abdomen and the slashes on my arms and chest.

"What happened, Sir?" she questioned while taking off her jacket. She set it on my trembling body and I answered,

"Some people tried to rob me. I tried to fight them, but..."

She smacked the side of my head before saying, "You don't fight robbers, Sir!"

"Please don't call me 'Sir',"

She looked me in the eye for a second before taking off her tee and using it to apply some pressure on my stab wound. "What is your name?"

"Chris," I answered. "Yours?"

She hesitated for a moment before answering, "Reed,"

I nodded and she sat on the ground beside me and supported my head. She pulled out her phone and called an ambulance. "You shouldn't stay here, Reed,"

"Why not?"

"It's not safe for a young girl like you, especially in the state you are in," I nodded pointedly towards her exposed chest and she gave an airy laugh.

"I have a gun. It wouldn't be safe to leave you all alone,"

And she stayed with me right up until the ambulance came. But just as I was about to explain to the paramedics and the police about the girl who had saved me, she was gone.

Disappeared into thin air.

I mentally slapped myself for being so slow. Ruth's maiden name was 'Reed'. She was Reed, she was the girl who had saved me.

I hadn't been able to remember her face given the loss of blood and the remnants of the alcohol in my blood, but it was all coming back to me.

The tee and jacket still tucked away someplace in my childhood house belonged to her. It all made suddenly made sense.

I had been attracted to her long before I had met her six months back. Ten years ago, when she had saved me and had shown me such kindness, I had fallen for her.

And perhaps, that was why we had chemistry. But one question remained in my mind: why didn't she remember me?

I spent the night on a chair beside Dante with my one hand gripping a fun.

I had as much faith in the E.Y.E facility as I did in the now rotting body of Adeline. None.

When I woke up the next morning, Ruth was already up and was having breakfast or at least something that she liked to call breakfast. All that I could see was a variety of seeds and some watermelon and a cucumber.

As I shifted on the chair, her eyes turned to me and she swallowed the bite that she was taking before asking me, "Why didn't you sleep elsewhere? You must've been terribly uncomfortable!"

I stretched my arms and my back before rising to my feet. "I don't trust this place. I couldn't leave you alone here while you were sedated and half dead," I answered and turned my attention to the plate in her hand. "You need to have actual food, you know that, right?"

"There's nothing wrong with this!"

"You have lost too much blood. Your body needs things to heal itself," she didn't argue with me, but didn't stop eating either.

I noticed that both Amara and Dante were gone. I walked over to her and put a palm against her head. I pulled it towards me and rested her head against my stomach.

She merely exhaled and closed her eyes before angling her head to have more comfort.

She pushed me away out of nowhere and looked away. "You have a girlfriend, Christian,"

Christian was playing with my feelings and I hated him for that. Why did he have to come back and make me remember the exact intensity of what I felt for him?

He was dating my employee, and what I felt for him was clearly one-sided, but I still couldn't configure his reasons for being so fiercely protective.

For flying to a different continent for me, for risking his life to fight against my enemy. It was more than complicated.

I owed him. A lot.

I was touched by his actions but at the same time, I couldn't help but feel *played*. He had no intention of being with me, so why would he do what he did?

I had no answers, so I did what I did best: I pushed him away and decided to kick him out of my life once and for all.

He had been awfully kind to me, but I didn't want to get hurt once more, I couldn't take it.

"I need to see Alex," I said once I realized that he wasn't satisfying my statement with a comment. He let my previous words hang in the air, completely ignoring them.

He helped me get up and helped me walk to Alex's room. Amara was already there, talking to Alex when we entered and Walker pulled back a chair for me to sit.

"Thanks, Walker," I murmured, my voice low. Amara took a seat beside me and I asked Alex, "How do you feel?"

"Better. What about you?"

"Great as usual,"

"The lack of handcuffs on my wrists is questionable," he joked and I chuckled.

"That was the part of the bargain. You and Amara are free to go anywhere you want. You'll have your new passports and identities. You can rejoin E.Y.E if you want but I suppose you have enough money to last you a lifetime so you can just buy a house in a small town and live there."

Alex opened his arms and I carefully pulled him in an embrace. His hold was full of need and love and I liked how it felt.

It had been a long time since anyone had held me that way.

He pulled back before saying, "Thank you so much, Ruth," I wanted to run a hand through his dark curls but his gaze shifted away as Amara left the room.

He turned his eyes back to me and secured my head in a firm hold before pulling me closer and kissing me slowly, softly, on the lips.

It was a small kiss, but it was intense enough to make me forget everything for a while.

It had been years since I had been kissed and even longer since I had been kissed with such passion.

I knew he had sensed the awkwardness between me and Christian and that he only wanted to help me make him jealous, but the kiss made me feel things I shouldn't.

In a span of fifteen minutes, I had been confused about my feelings for two entirely different men, I had felt more than I had in the past five years.

"Thank you," I whispered in a low voice so only he could hear.

The room succumbed to awkward silence before Alexander decided to break it by saying, "I'll always be in your debt, Ruth. Whenever you need..."

"I'll come find you," I finished his sentence because I knew him well enough to know what he would offer. But to be honest, I didn't want to have to find him because I didn't want to lose him in the first place.

Nonetheless, I left the room, unable to sit in the presence of two of my crushes.

Christian didn't say anything but I think he got the hint. I didn't want to hurt him, I just wanted to decide what he wanted.

The next few days passed at the E.Y.E facility. Christian left once he was certain that I was okay. Dante, Alex, and Amara kept me occupied and Caeser dropped in from time to time.

To say that I was relieved to leave the place would be an understatement. I hadn't seen my daughter in a long time, plus I had a lot of work to do.

The only thing left to do was talk to Alex, a conversation that I had been avoiding despite how much I looked forward to it.

He had healed up well by the time we had decided to go back. His skin had almost developed back up and the scars were vanishing.

I was still in a pretty fragile state. My stab wounds had started healing but they weren't completely gone. The mouse hadn't damaged any organs but it had torn apart several muscles in my abdomen.

My broken rib had healed faster than I had originally guessed which was good cause I got the permission to walk around.

However, I still had a long way to go before the doctor allowed me to do any sort of exercise.

Alejandro felt immensely guilty for what Adeline had done to me, and I felt guilty for what Adeline had done to him, so, I decided to make it up to him in the best way I could.

I knocked once before entering his room. He had a glass of bourbon in his hand with two empty bottles on the table. One day, his liver was going to fail, I was certain of it.

He was so used to drinking all the time that despite how much he had consumed, he wasn't even close to drunk.

I took the glass from his hand and poured its contents into the bin. He didn't argue, nor did he bother to fight me. He knew it was of no use.

He only lifted his eyebrows in amusement before asking me what was wrong.

"You have a daughter to take care of and you need to live long enough for that,"

He reached out a hand and wrapped it around my waist and suddenly pulled me closer, grabbing my head. "You need to stop looking after me," he said, his voice rough and husky.

"Why?" I asked him, my heart beating out of my chest at the close proximity.

He leaned and craned his neck to touch his forehead to mine. He closed his eyes and inhaled deeply before opening them again.

The green orbs mesmerized me enough to make me inch my face closer to him, letting my lips hover right below his.

I was scared. I was scared that he would push me away, that he didn't like me that way, but he pressed his lips to mine.

He didn't move them, as if he was still considering take-backs. I pulled back a little before saying, "Your wife just died,"

Apparently, that did something to him because he tightened his grip on my waist and he brought his lips back down to mine and kissed me roughly.

In a second, all of my hesitation melted away and I got on my tiptoes and kissed him back. His hand on my waist lowered to my hips and he cleared the table of all the bottles, letting them crash on the floor with the rest of the stuff before lifting me up and setting me on the table, all while not breaking the kiss.

His hand on my head lowered to my neck and then he used both of his hands to hold my shoulders and I winced as one of his hands came in contact with my injured shoulder.

He immediately pulled back and I could feel him getting his senses back from the look in his eyes. "Are you okay?" He checked my top to make sure that I wasn't bleeding.

"I am fine,"

He sighed in relief before letting his head drop. "I am so sorry. I completely-"

"It's okay, Alex, I am fine!" I reassured him, trying to smile through the pain slowly building up.

He kissed my cheek tenderly before tucking a strand of my hair behind my ear. "So, why were you here?" he asked as if we just hadn't made out.

"I want you to come with me. To my place. There are a lot of homes and I can have a place for you ready elsewhere but until then, I want you to stay with me,"

His eyes glinted. "You shouldn't make such proposals, especially when you aren't ready to face the consequences of them," he warned in a deep voice before winking.

I shoved his chest playfully before asking, "So you'll come, right?"

"I don't know how to pay you back for all this, though,"

"You don't have to," I meant it. I would've done a lot more for him without even blinking much less thinking about repayment.

He looked at me sincerely for a moment before nodding. "Thank you so much, Ruth,"

I smiled up at him and I felt like I was eighteen again, the same naïve little girl who had fallen in love with a boy who would always love her, but would never learn how to show it.

Alex wasn't like Ryan, he wasn't abusive or egoistic, at least not when it came to the people he loved, but that still didn't make him the right choice.

His wife had just died, he was looking for a rebound and I was voluntarily offering to be the pig for slaughter and all because Alex and I had always had chemistry, we had always had something more.

Alex joined me on my flight back. He had some of his belongings, but there weren't too many pairs of clothes with the two of them.

I had Emily, my assistant, pick out clothes for the two of them and have them sent to my house. My former mother-in-law, Bianca, got to my place with Leah before I reached home and had the housekeeper clean everything up and prepare two rooms for Amara and Alejandro.

She was waiting for me in the living room when I got home and I had no clue how to thank her for all that she had done.

She had helped me more than my own parents had, and there was nothing I could ever do to repay her. In my small attempts to pay her back, I monthly sent her vouchers and gift cards for different places. I knew she would never take any money from me, so, all I could do was pay her that way.

After her husband and she had gotten divorced which was my fault, she had gone into a bit of a financial crisis. She had gotten a house and a lot of money, but she didn't have any sort of income to maintain her house.

With her son in prison, she had no one to help her, so, I had started looking out for her. I had scheduled monthly visits from the plumbers, carpenters, electricians, and housekeepers and sent her groceries every two weeks.

Luckily, when she got divorced, my company was already well-established, so, spending all that money created no issues for me, but it made a huge difference to her. Also, if I hadn't been in her life, her son wouldn't have landed in prison, and her husband wouldn't have divorced her.

Things would've been different for her, better for her.

But, to be honest, she didn't see things that way, and I suppose that was what made her so great.

And if that wasn't enough, she had spent weeks taking care of Leah. Leah wasn't an easy kid to look after. She wasn't mischievous, but she had her own sort of tantrums every once in a while.

She was my daughter, and so, naturally, she had inherited my attitude, my ego, and if they weren't enough, both her father's and I's temper.

7
Christian

————◦♡◦————

I had waited for a few days for Ruth to heal before leaving. She had moved on, she had found another guy, and she had replaced what I could've been to her, and it was all my fault.

Spending those days with her, I had realized that she made me feel the way no one else ever did. Her presence made me feel content, happy, and calm. I didn't usually have to think twice before speaking in front of her.

She put me at ease and made me feel comfortable, and I knew it was because subconsciously, I had always known that she was the one.

I waited to go back before cutting things off with Julia, she didn't deserve to get broken up over a call.

I asked her to meet me the day I landed. I was tired and exhausted and I had no strength left for a break-up, but would I sound like a total jerk if I were to accept that I didn't want to wait for even a minute anymore?

I thought I really liked Julia but the second I met Ruth again, it was as if anything that I felt was any other person was rudimentary, vestigial, and not visceral.

With Ruth it was natural. I felt protective of that girl, I felt like even though I didn't know her, I did know her.

As if I had fallen in love with her and not seeing her for six months had only intensified that love.

The last time, I had lied to her, had gone behind her back, and had almost gotten her killed.

She hated me for that, of course, she did, and I didn't blame her at all. I deserved to be hated for all I had done.

It was just that behind all that hatred, I could see that she liked me, or at least I had hoped that she did. All that hope had been torn away when I had seen her kiss Alejandro, and that too in front of me.

I could tell that Alejandro had only kissed her to make me jealous, I knew that was the intention, but honestly, there was a lot behind that kiss. I knew that they weren't lovers, but the way chemistry sizzled between them, I knew that they could be.

Ruth kept on smiling to herself after their exchange and I deserved it after dating her employee but it certainly didn't feel good.

In those moments, I had realized that being with any other girl would not justice to that girl, at least not until I sorted out all my emotions.

So, I invited myself to Julia's house, so that I could leave without knowing that she wouldn't drive while crying or while being drunk. That way, she won't have to drive.

In six months, Julia and I hadn't yet gotten to the 'I love you' part. I had sensed that she wanted me to say it first, but I had never been able to find the right moment to say it so I would mean it.

I had spent the last six months keeping an eye on Ruth. Not exactly stalking but I think what I did was somewhere along the lines of stalking.

The guilt had started to eat me alive so at first it had started as a way of knowing that she was okay and then it became a habit.

I didn't usually use my abilities to do wrong, but for my satisfaction, I had hacked the cameras around her house. I didn't go as far as to invade her privacy, I just kept an eye on her and made sure no one broke inside her house.

We usually had coffee from the same place, so, I had a few tables away from the counter and watched as she took her macchiato on the go.

I usually did my morning walk by following her to her house. She usually walked back home unless on some rare occasions during which she was late. I hired one of Dante's men to make sure that Leah was fine at her school while I hacked the cameras outside Ruth's office.

At night, when Ruth left to get back home I discreetly followed her with my car to be certain that she was okay.

A month later, it became a schedule.

When I couldn't follow her, I had one of my most trusted men do it. She wasn't a bad person, she just had some deep baggage, and a lot of past trauma. She bossed around and showed her attitude, but it was a defense mechanism to hide her vulnerability, to hide how easily she could be hurt like I had hurt her.

I had hurt her once, I had hurt her twice and then, I had hurt her a third time, and I wanted to spend the rest of my life making amends.

Julia was waiting for me patiently, but she didn't hug me the second I entered, she didn't tell me how much she missed me.

She placed a hand on my cheek and kissed the other one before grabbing my hand and pulling me inside. "We need to talk,"

The tone of her voice conveyed exactly what she wanted to express. She wanted to break up with me, and I was relieved that I wasn't the one doing so.

Her house was big for a single person to live in. It had three bedrooms, one of which she had turned into a closet, a dining room, a living room, and two bathrooms, and it wasn't just huge, it was beautiful.

Her sense of interior was just as good as her sense of fashion.

She had a knack for things like that, and a good choice, of course, it was obvious from the fact that she had chosen me.

She handed me a cup of coffee: black, just as I liked it. I let the hot liquid warm my throat which suddenly felt funny.

She stood in front of me while I sat on a stool in front of the island. She poured herself a glass of water and eyed me carefully.

"We need to talk,"

It wasn't me who said those words, it was her, and I suddenly felt aware of how small her eyes looked. The bags under them were dark and prominent and she definitely looked like she had been crying.

Remorse crept up on me and I realized where the conversation was heading.

"What happened between you and Mrs Diaz?" the way she used such respect for Ruth despite what happened, touched me. "Not in the past week but back before we started dating,"

I wasn't a liar, so I came clean, "We had chemistry, I guess. I never really knew why, but her personality was just so alluring. I asked her out but then I thought that she was a slut, so I canceled the date. We just flirted a little and got to that phase before dating but then I met you. I realized that no matter how nice Ruth was, she had too many men in her life and I needed someone loyal like you,"

"So, you asked me out without thinking twice about Mrs Diaz?

"I seriously thought that she was just playing around,"

She looked for the truth in my eyes but I think she found a truth that was even worse.

"You still like her, don't you?" her voice broke and I felt awful for what I had done to her.

"She saved my life ten years ago," I said quietly.

"We need to break up," she wasn't saying those words to me, she was saying them to her own self. We did need to break up, but for me, that would mean going back after Ruth. And for her, it meant going through a bad break-up.

I had loved Julia, I did love her even then, but despite what time I had spent with her in the past six months, what I felt for Ruth still overpowered that.

I nodded and stood up before putting the half-consumed mug filled with coffee on the island. Her eyes trailed my movements before a tear escaped them. She let it flow and she looked as though she had zoned out.

I wiped the tear with a finger and pressed a kiss on her cheek. "I am sorry,"

She didn't lie and assure me that it was okay. It wasn't okay, what I had done was horrible.

I had played with her feelings and had let her believe that I loved her all the while I was in love with Ruth, and I didn't even know about that.

"I promise I'll make it up to you someday," and I meant it. I hated myself for what I had done to her, and I wanted to try my best to make it better.

I left to give her some space, but I am not proud of what I did next. I drove to Ruth's mother-in-law's place to meet Leah.

Bianca was a warm lady and she knew me from our previous encounter, so, she didn't hesitate to let me inside.

She called Leah out who squealed on seeing me. I was happy to see that girl as well. She had so much attitude for a five-year-old that it was actually cute and what was even cuter was how often she dropped that attitude.

"How are you, Leah?" I asked after picking her up in my arms.

"I am awesome, as usual," I smiled at her response and set her on the couch. "Why didn't you visit us for so long?" she asked me, pouting.

I chuckled, trying to conceal the reality behind it. "I was busy, I am so sorry. But now, I want to make it up to you and your mother,"

"You messed up, didn't you?" she asked and I frowned. "Mom didn't let me invite you to my birthday, so I figured," she explained.

"You're smart for your age,"

"I know," the similarity of her responses to Ruth's made me smile. "What help do you want?"

I explained it all to her. I asked her everything: from Ruth's favorite flower to place. I wanted to make it perfect, and I wasn't sparing any effort in doing so.

The plan we came up with was simple. I would wait for her at her house and when she'd come, I would give her a rose that looked the closest to black.

I would take her to see a movie, drive her to her favorite restaurant, and then take her to my cottage beside a lake in the woods where I would tell her how I felt.

It wasn't something extra, nothing cringe or nothing that would make her run in the other direction. Ruth Diaz had a hard time accepting love and grand gestures, so I had to come up with a small one.

The day came sooner than I had expected. Just as I had planned, I wanted in front of her house, hidden in the trees. I watched as her car pulled up along with the other cars for her safety, but she didn't get down from it.

Instead, Alejandro appeared, and he helped her out of the car gently. Amara, his daughter, followed them, and I assumed that he was there to stay until he got a place of his own.

The guards took her belongings inside and Alejandro asked Amara to go in as well.

As soon as everyone left, I decided to leave my hideout but before I could do so, I noticed the awkwardness in the air.

Ruth looked...shy and hesitant but the tension melted away the second Alex grabbed her waist and pulled her closer. Tenderly, but roughly at the same time, he spun her around so that her back was pressed against the wall around her house and he kissed her firmly.

Ruth grabbed the back of his neck and kissed him back with the same passion and I felt like someone had crushed my heart under their feet.

The rose in my hand fell to the ground and I felt myself crumbled. My heart physically hurt and I clenched my chest, trying not to feel any pain as I saw the two of them together.

I hadn't known her for too long, I shouldn't have felt so much pain, but oddly, I did. I turned back around and disappeared into the small patch of woods surrounding her house, on the other side of which was my car.

The branches were sharp, but I couldn't care less for any injuries, much less my suit. I unlocked my car and got into the driving seat before letting the road take me.

I didn't want to go back home, the place which was all blue and lonely with no one else inside, the place from where Julia had probably taken away her belongings.

So I took the highway and drove all the way to my sister's house which was in the town beside mine.

Sarah was only three years older than me, but she was already married and had two kids. She had a stable life, a proper lifestyle, and a happy family, so, I knew I could rely on her and visit her anytime I wanted.

Ava, though, was five years younger than me, and her life was…adventurous. Ava liked drinking, partying out till late, and drowning herself in music and booze until everything seemed right in her world.

She was doing masters in fashion designing, a branch she loved more than anything. She wasn't one to have one partner, one man, she had a list of lovers, from several countries in the world.

Ava was wild, but she was also tired of life, and I couldn't be a burden to her until she got her own thing together.

By the time I reached Sarah's place, my tie was on the mat of the car, my sleeves were rolled up and my shirt's first two buttons were undone.

I hadn't realized when exactly I had managed to wreck myself, but somewhere along the way, I had started feeling suffocated and the result was a mess.

I had blasted the music at the full volume, not allowing myself to think or to feel until I got there. She was supposed to be just a crush, and crushes shouldn't affect you like that, right?

But no, she wasn't just a crush, I knew that deep inside my heart from the moment I had met her seven months ago.

I rang the doorbell, hoping to get some answers from my sister. Sarah knew everything there was about love. She was the cupid in school having met the love of her life at seven. She matched people up with her experience and expertise.

Sarah had to know where I was stuck.

She opened the door, and her face changed from happiness to shock to panic in a matter of three seconds.

"What happened, Chris?" she asked, opening the door wider to let me in.

I numbly walked inside, my mind focused on a thousand things at once, and all of them about Ruth: from her fake laugh to her beautiful, real smile to her smirk, it all echoed inside my head.

Sarah's older kid Jay got me a glass of water, but he was smart not to ask me any questions. Sarah took a seat beside me on the couch and softly put an arm on my shoulder.

"Christian?" she called and her voice slowly broke me out of my trance. I dropped my head on her shoulder and she pulled me closer, rubbing my back.

"I don't know what's wrong, Sar," I said, letting the timidness from all the past few months take over.

"Do you want to talk about it?" I nodded and she pulled away a little so that she could look me in the eyes. "What happened, Chris?"

"You remember how I almost died on the street ten years ago?" I asked and she nodded. "I met the girl who saved my life,"

"Who is she?" she immediately asked.

"Ruth. Ruth Diaz,"

And then, I told her everything from the beginning, even the bad parts and especially the rough ones. Normally, she would've hit me if she had found out that I had called a girl a slut by being over-presumptuous, but she knew that I regretted it enough, so she kept quiet about that.

When I was done, she grabbed my face and looked me straight into my eyes, my soul, before declaring, "Christian Walker, you're in love,"

8
Ruth

Things between me and Alex were weird the first night that he stayed over. We had kissed multiple times and I suppose it meant that we were a thing but there was nothing official yet and it scared me.

Alex sensed my discomfort on the drive home and he did his best to try to ease me, but when nothing worked, he asked me out on a date with both of our daughters present since he couldn't leave Amara alone for a minute.

I liked it because of how serious it sounded, and even though it wasn't actually a date, it felt just as intimate if not more.

I put on one of my favorite dresses: a black halter neck with a slit that was a little too high.

It was daring and that was what I loved the most about it.

I put on a pair of stilettoes and a diamond set before walking outside the house. Alex was coming out with the girls while I was getting the car ready, double-checking the security of everything.

A tiny detail caught my eye: a rose which wasn't there before. It was lying almost opposite to the gate on the floor and it didn't look old. The thing was that no one had come to see me. I knelt but before I could pick it up, Alex's voice came from behind me, calling my name.

"What happened?" he asked and I rose quickly, turned towards him, and closed my legs to subtly hide the flower from him.

He didn't suspect anything. He smiled and pressed a kiss to my cheek and I blushed.

Alex was a little possessive, at least with Antsiyanah he was. If he were to find a rose outside my house, he would find the person responsible and kill him, and something told me that I wasn't going to like Christian dead.

It was obvious that it was him. He was one of the very few people with the ability to breach my security and appear there.

But the fact that he had come to my place with a red rose made me realize his intentions. It meant that he had ended things with Julia and was there to ask me out.

Treacherous butterflies jumped in my stomach, and I felt guilty for feeling things for him while being with Alexander, but I pushed the remorse to the back of my mind and instead, focused on the moment.

I loved Alex, maybe I could *fall* in love with him as well and he could be the one.

It was sick that I was dating my dead best friend's ex-husband but she had moved on from Alex a long time ago. A part of her had loved him even as she died, but her love had been broken down, had shattered into pieces especially after Alex killed her husband, so, her hate and need had taken control, suppressing the remnants of love.

She didn't love Alex much, she needed him to save their daughter from E.Y.E and Adeline and that was the only reason she wanted him. Maybe she did want to see her first love for one last time but I refused to believe that she still loved him as much as before.

So, I was in clear. The only issue was Alex's possessiveness which could lead to him killing a large number of people on the planet, and one of them who I liked very much.

I needed to talk about that with Alex and make sure that he wouldn't harm Christian. Christian was strong and smart, perhaps even as much as Alex, but I never wanted to put him in a situation where his life would be in jeopardy.

Alex took my hand in his and walked the three of us to the car waiting outside.

He had Amara and Leah sit in the back and he opened the passenger seat to let me in.

I closed the door and he sat in the driver's seat and the engine revved to life. I put on my seatbelt and Alex did the same and it took me a moment to feel the tension radiating from him.

I looked at him expectingly, waiting for him to say something back but he remained quiet. "What happened?" I asked and he changed the gear audibly, making me flinch and scoot away slightly.

His jaw clenched but he didn't say anything. I decided to push it by calling out his name.

He harshly ran over a bump and my voice grew louder, "Alex!"

He pressed the brakes suddenly and roughly turned to me, making me inch away and press my back to the door.

I was strong, I was an E.Y.E agent and a good one at that, one of the best actually. I wasn't scared of Alex, it's just his attitude brought back bad memories, memories that Alex knew about.

His demeanor softened but his voice remained hard as he asked, "Who gave you the rose, Ruth?"

"I don't know. Someone left it there!" I replied honestly, and I felt my fear slowly subside. I could fight him, couldn't I?

No, he had more muscles and more strength, and I had no weapons on me because he had offered to carry them. I was unarmed, and-

"I am not Ryan," he whispered softly in Italian as he realized exactly what I was calculating. "I am not going to hit you,"

"Really? Cause for a second right there it looked like you were," I got the nerve to shoot back. His daughter was in the back seat and while we could argue in Italian, he could never hit me.

He buried his face in his hands as he realized his mistake. "I am so sorry, I forgot for a second that-" he cut himself off at the right moment and I unbuckled my seatbelt.

"You forgot what? That I wasn't tough?" I wasn't looking for a reason to fight, but to be honest, I trusted Alex to keep my past in mind.

Yes, it had happened a long time ago, but it had also happened the last time I had fallen in love.

I unlocked the door desperate in need of some fresh air. "Ruth wait," Alex urged, but I was in no mood to listen.

"Don't stop me, Alex," he hesitated for a moment but he knew me and my tendencies and how I needed space almost all the time. "Take them to dinner. I'll walk back home,"

He nodded and I walked out of the car. Just as I was about to close the door, I saw him reach out a gun towards me. "Keep it with you and be safe,"

I took the gun from his hand but didn't grace him with an answer. Instead, I closed the door and started walking back towards my house and Alex drove in the opposite direction.

I had only just started walking when I saw the headlights of a car approaching me from behind. Assuming it was Alex, I stomped my foot and turned around, only to find a different car coming towards me.

Instinctively, my hands reached for the gun and I was about to pull it out when I noticed the number plate. I relaxed, and instead of running in the opposite direction, I walked right towards my dearest and most favorite stalker.

I folded my arms with the attitude of a preteen and waited for him to explain himself.

Christian got out of the car and in a single phrase, said all that he needed to, "Get in,"

He looked attractive as hell in his grey shirt and black suit and I almost couldn't refuse him.

"I would, but I don't want Alex to kill you. Dante would have to find another partner and then I would need to give him a lot of emotional support and it will be a whole thing, so, unfortunately, I'll pass."

Christian gave me a look before saying, "I'll take my chances,"

I scoffed, "No way in hell am *I* taking any chances,"

He sighed before locking the car and making his way towards me.

"What are you doing?" I asked as he took off his jacket.

"You won't get inside, so, I will just walk you home," he answered before draping his blazer over my shoulders. He tenderly grabbed ahold of my hand and my heart jumped out of my chest as he helped me get it through the sleeves.

Our eyes locked for a moment making me go batshit crazy but he didn't hold my gaze. Instead, he put my hand through the other sleeve before turning around and locking the car.

"You don't have to come. I have a gun with me, I'll be perfectly safe,"

He grinned at me before ruffling my hair a little and saying, "I have three. The more the merrier, right?"

I didn't argue, but looking at his carefree face and boyish grin, I couldn't help but smile.

His expression turned a little serious as he asked, "He didn't hurt you, right?"

I shook my head. Alex would never hurt me, that I knew for sure. I trusted him at least that much.

"You're too trusting," I hadn't heard those words in the past few years for me and they made my heart curl. He was probably right, I was making the same mistake that I had made with Ryan. His gaze softened as he noticed the look in my eyes and he spoke sincerely, "If he does hurt you, Ruth, tell me. Please,"

I wanted to tell him that I was capable of taking care of myself, but I just nodded before drifting away in my thoughts.

"I am sorry," he said out of nowhere and I turned my head to look up at him. He looked back at me from behind his soft light brown lashes that were long enough to make me jealous.

"For?" I asked, making him stop walking and I followed the suite.

He turned to me and my breathing hitched at how perfect he looked under the lamplight. "For starters, calling you a slut," he paused for a second before continuing. "For not telling you about the plan and almost getting you killed," his next pause was longer. "And most of all, for dating your employee,"

I looked away from him before muttering and resuming my walk, "You have nothing to apologize for,"

In an attempt to stop me, raised his arm and put it gently in front of my body. It didn't touch me, but I guessed that the point was to not touch me, so he wouldn't scare me.

Normally, I would've hated him for treating me like glass, but at that moment, I needed to be treated like that. I was already reliving my moments with Ryan, and the last thing I needed was a man grabbing me from behind.

"Please don't pretend, my diamond,"

The nickname made me smile, but it didn't bring me out of denial, "You really have nothing to apologize for, my dearest stalker,"

He chuckled, momentarily looking at his feet. "I know I messed up, Diaz, but I promise that if you were to give me another chance that I know I don't deserve, I'll make it up to you,"

He sounded like he meant it, but I had already given him three chances: all of which he had thrown away. I didn't have it in me to trust him again.

"Look, Christian, you don't have to apologize for anything. You have already made it up for it by looking after me for the past six months,"

"You know..." he whispered.

"Yes, of course, I know. I have known about you following me since the first day. I am an agent, I have been trained my whole life for this," I knew he followed me to my coffee shop and then back to my house. I knew he had eyes on me when I was at work and when I returned. I knew that he had hacked into all those cameras. I knew it all. "And I have felt extremely safe knowing that you were out there.

But this has to end. I.." I exhaled before continuing. "I am with Alex now. So, you don't have to worry. He can take care of me,"

"He almost hit you, Ruth!" he snapped.

" 'Almost, is the keyword! He didn't actually do it!"

"I am sure you made the same excuses for you your ex-husband!" I was certain that he regretted saying those words as soon as they left his mouth. "Ruth-" he tried to make it better as he noticed the hurt in my eyes but I put a hand between us to tell him to stop.

"Give me a gun," I ordered, holding out a hand. He did so without hesitating. "I am leaving and if you follow me this time, I will shoot you with your own gun!" I threatened before taking off in the direction of my house.

He followed. He maintained a distance between the two of us, but he followed without hesitation.

I ignored him and forced my eyes to suck in the tears that were about to make their way out.

I attempted to walk faster and twisted my ankle in the process. The crack was audible enough to make Christian rush to my side from ten feet behind me.

"I am fine," I protested, forcing myself away from him. Luckily for me, my house was only ten steps away. I removed my stilettoes and walked the last ten steps with them in my hand.

As soon as a guard saw me limping, he helped me walk inside, and I didn't look back once at the figure of Christian at the gate.

Bianca had left by the time I got inside, which was fortunate since I had no intention of tending to my injury.

All I wanted to do was close my eyes and escape to a land where I hadn't married the wrong guy, and so, that was exactly what I did.

9

Ruth

Alex had returned with the girls when I woke up. I realized that he had moved me to my bed from the couch and had covered me with a blanket, though, much to my dismay, he hadn't taken it upon himself to change my clothes.

He was sitting on the edge of my bed as if waiting eagerly for me to open my eyes. "Hey," he whispered softly as I rose. "I am so sorry for what happened, Ruth. I didn't mean to react that way, it's just-"

"Who you are, Alex. I know your temper. I am sorry for being dramatic. As long as you don't hurt me, I am ready to accept you for who you are,"

He smiled at me and I noticed the dryness under his eyes that showed that he had been crying.

"Let's get some sleep," I suggested, getting to my feet. I had completely forgotten about the pain in my ankle and would've collapsed if it weren't for Alex.

"What happened?" he asked concerningly.

"I twisted my ankle," I answered and he slowly made me sit down and knelt in front of me.

He took off his tie and slowly wrapped the silky material around my throbbing ankle. I gulped as the air thickened with tension and he rested his hand on the skin of my thigh exposed by the slit.

"How much does it hurt?" he asked huskily.

"Not enough," I replied, my voice barely louder than a whisper.

"Good," he said, crashing his lips into mine. "Good," he repeated.

Half my muscles were dead by the time I woke up the next morning. I was a trained agent and worked out twice a day, but half my muscles had still spasmed.

The light coming from the windows pierced my eyes making me crawl back under the sheets.

"You're up," came Alex's voice. I peeked from under the sheets and saw him standing near my table while holding a cup of coffee. He was only wearing sweatpants and his hair was wet and the water trickled down his bare chest as he made his way towards me.

"That was the best sex I have ever had," escaped my mouth before I could stop myself and I covered my mouth in embarrassment.

He chuckled before answering, "That would've been a compliment if the only person you had slept with apart from me wouldn't have been your shitty excuse of a husband,"

I pulled myself into a sitting position, ignoring the aching muscles of my back. The tie that earlier worked as a bandage, had taken a new function of working as a blindfold at the beginning, and it now laid pooled over my collar bones at the base of my neck.

I took it off and offered it to him but instead of taking it from my hands his hand grabbed my chin and forced me to look up at him in the eyes.

My eyes widened and I was about to protest and claim that I was still sore when he grumbled, "You used me,"

I grabbed his hand by the wrist in a threatening hold and he let go of my wrist. "What are you talking about?"

"Christian was smart enough to delete all the footage of last night, but what he didn't do was take care of the guard who found you. It took some...persuasion, but he finally told me who you had come home with,"

Persuasion was another word for torture, but I decided to take care of that later.

"Why were you checking the footage?"

"I wanted to know how you hurt your ankle," he replied, reaching out underneath the sheets to pull out my injured leg. He kissed it from my knee to my ankle while saying, "Because the Ruth I know doesn't trip while wearing stilettoes,"

He pushed me back down and was about the pull away the sheet entirely but I put a hand on his chest to stop him. He came to his senses immediately and I pleaded, "Please don't hurt him,"

His hand enclosed mine that was on his chest and he kissed my knuckles. He brought his lips down to my neck and kissed his way to my clavicle and I shut my eyes and realized that it was the price I was going to pay to keep Christian alive.

Alex must've sensed that something was wrong because he immediately pulled back. I opened my eyes and he grabbed the sheets and wrapped them around me more securely.

He tenderly took a hold of my face and kissed my forehead. "Get dressed, Ruth,"

I waited for him to leave before getting to my feet only to find that the pain in my ankle had almost vanished. I dropped the sheet and walked to the bathroom, knowing well that no one would enter the room.

I hopped into the shower and let the warm water soothe my sore muscles. When I got out of the shower, I took a moment to survey myself in the mirror.

I had bruises and hickeys covering the better part of my body, and I knew for a fact, that they were only going to get darker.

I picked out a full-sleeved turtleneck black top and a pair of treggings for the day. I used make-up to hide the faint mark on my face before pulling my hair into a bun for convenience and making my way to Alex and the girls.

They were all waiting for me at the table. Amara and Leah seemed to get along just fine by the looks of it, and a day ago, I would've been glad, but at that moment, I felt nothing.

"Aunt Ruth?" Amara called, pulling me out of my thoughts.

"Yes, darling?"

"I think there's a ghost in your house," my eyes widened. I didn't believe in ghosts, but I didn't like that something had scared the little girl in my house.

"Why, sweetheart, what happened?" I asked her, taking her face in my hand.

"I heard a woman scream dad's name all night long last night,"

I blanched and Alex choked on his toast. He burst out laughing and I shot him a glare before soothing Amara, "Don't worry, Amara, it was nothing. There are no ghosts here,"

Amara nodded. I grabbed Alex by his arm and forced him to get up and took him to a secluded area. "This is all your fault," I accused him, jabbing a finger at his chest.

"Oh please, you weren't complaining last night,"

I smacked his arm and he snacked an arm around my waist and pulled me closer. "What's on your mind, Ruth?"

I gently pushed him away and asked, "What did you mean when said that I used you?"

His gaze fell to the ground and my heart clenched in anticipation. He knew. Last night, the truth that I had found out, he had found out as well.

"You don't love me, Reed," he said, kissing my forehead. "And you never will. I don't think I'll love you that way either. You're in love with Christian, and honestly, I think you two are meant to be,"

"Alex-"

"I am a rough man, Ruth, I have never learned how to treat a woman right. Antsiyanah knew that about me and I think she liked it. But you, Reed, you are delicate in the most beautiful way. We won't work out, Ruth,"

He was right, we would never work out. There was no way I could play that rough for the rest of my life. Even without my past, I always craved softness. That was just who I was.

So, I nodded, and he told me that he would be gone by the evening and that he and Amara would find a place to stay and I was fine.

But I was on a mission though, a mission to get Christian Walker.

He had expressed his love for me, he had offered to go out with me indirectly and he would be okay if I were to take up on his offer, right?

I went to grab my coffee, and just like I had expected, he was there. I was late because of my conversation with Alex, but he was right at the door, holding my drink.

I wordlessly took it from his hands and we silently walked back to my home. I wasn't playing hard to get, but for once, after years, I had no clue what to say to a boy.

Luckily, I was meeting Dante at his office in a few hours, and I was certain that I would meet Christian since they were on the same floor.

I drove to my office first and sorted everything out before driving to Dante's office.

My brother hadn't picked out a cringe name for his company like 'Fortress Services' or 'SafeHaven Services'. Originally, the name was 'Vigilance' but after merging with Christian's company, they had settled on a simple name, 'C & D'.

It was stupid, childish and perhaps 'Walker and Reed' would've sounded far better, but the thing was that Dante hated how his surname connected him to our parents.

He and I had severed the link with our parents right after my divorce. While I had stuck to 'Diaz', my husband's surname, because it was on too many legal documents related to the company and because I hated our parents almost as much as I hated my husband, Dante had no such practical option.

Often, he had considered just changing it, but he had never been able to find something that fit. A name that made him feel like himself.

So, all I could do was stare at the logo of C & D while the receptionist logged my entry.

It didn't take long, since they all knew me, and in a matter of seconds, they all helped me inside and Dante's assistant led me to his office.

With my luck, Christian was inside and they were casually talking when I entered.

Christian stopped whatever he was saying and turned to look at me. His blue eyes sent electric waves down my body, making me shiver.

Dante must've noticed the chemistry in the air because he waited for it to subside before saying anything. "How are you doing, Ruth?" he asked me and I smiled before answering,

"Wonderful," and I genuinely meant it. All I needed to do was confess my love for Christian in a way that wouldn't send him running and we'd be fine.

"Nothing hurts, right?" I shook my head in response and he sighed in relief. "Water?" he offered and I nodded.

"I'll get it," I reached out to grab the jug and poured myself a glass of water.

"What's that?" Dante asked when he noticed the skin of my wrist exposed. For a moment, I was confused as to what he was referring to.

But he made his way to me and rolled my sleeve up to examine what had caught his eyes and I realized how much in trouble I was.

Marks of the rope used to tie my curtains were there cause of how hard Alex had bound me the previous night, but before I could give him a sign, his eyes jumped to my neck.

"Why is your neck covered as well?" he questioned suspiciously and rolled down my turtle neck a little, exposing the bright red fingerprints there. "What happened, Ruth?" he asked before he noticed what I assumed was a bright red hickey. "Ohhh..." his voice trailed off as he realized what the cause of the marks was. My brother was protective, but he didn't intervene much in my almost nonexistent sex life. He chuckled, and turned toward Christian before joking, "I didn't know you were in this kind of stuff, man,"

The temperature dropped a hundred degrees as Christian surveyed me with his gaze hard. "I am not," was all he said before walking out of the office aggressively.

Dante turned to me and asked, "Why would you do that, Ruth?" I had no explanation, no justification and Dante lost it. "You find one nice guy and you drive him away, Ruth?"

"Dante, I-"

"No, don't even bother! I have always sided with you. Always. But what you did was bitchy and you were every bit of a *whore* you want people to believe,"

I ran out of his office before he could apologize or say something to make it better. Without bothering to knock, I barged into Christian's office, only to find him sitting on his couch drowning down what I assumed was vodka.

His tie was loosely hanging from his neck. His jacket was still on, but the first three buttons of his shirt were undone. He would've been the most beautiful thing on the planet at that moment for me had he not been mad at me.

"I broke things off with Alex," I blurted and he only gave a wry look in response. "I am sorry, Christian, I really am."

"I don't know who I am mad at, Ruth. I thought I would be able to take you being with another man but then I saw his marks on your body and..." his voice trailed off and he rested his head in his hands after putting away the glass of vodka he was holding. "I can't...I can't do this..."

"Christian, I am sorry, I ended things with him. It was a mistake-"

"Don't apologize Ruth. I dated Julia: what I did was worse. The thing is that we are both confused and I don't want to jump into something both of us aren't a hundred percent certain about,"

He was right, he was so right, but it still hurt. I took a step back, and then another, and another, until he was out of my sight and then all I did was jump in my car.

I forced myself to hold it together until I reached the comfort of my home, and once I did, I collapsed on the floor as the pain in my chest became unbearable.

I wasn't sure whether I was hyperventilating or if something was actually wrong with my heart, but I realized that it was the latter when I crumbled down, unable to take in any breaths.

I grabbed my phone but in the moment of hesitation about who to reach out to, darkness crawled in and I blacked out.

When I woke up, I was right when I had fainted. Much time hadn't passed and I noticed that Leah wasn't home yet which was good since the last thing I wanted was her to see her mom knocked out on the floor.

The housekeeper had perhaps yet to clean my room, so if she hadn't noticed me.

With great effort, I got to my feet and swore to myself to never fall in love again.

10

Christian

———❦———

3 months later

Drake was standing right beside me, and a sense of déjà vu took over me as he mentioned that Ruth was fashionably late.

The hollow in my chest intensified as I stared at the door, a part of me hoping that she wouldn't come. I didn't know whether I would be able to stand her presence, especially after our last encounter.

I had almost gotten her, but I had been so damn stupid to tell her to go away. As much as I regretted my decision, I knew it was the right thing to do.

Clicking of heels in a nearby distance helped me brace for when Ruth entered my office.

She looked completely different from the way she did the last time I had seen her. Her bangs were gone and she had cut her hair to her shoulder.

She didn't have a smirk on her face, there wasn't a smile either. Her face was blank: showing no expressions, and the attitude in her walk had disappeared.

She looked like a queen who had all the power in the world but no reason to wield it.

Her eyes gave away nothing as they met mine. There was no familiarity, no warmth in them, just pure indifference.

I rose and reached out a hand towards her and she shook it, but her move didn't drip with dominance like it had when I had seen her first in her office. Her grip was light and weightless.

"Please sit," I said, hoping to hear something in return but she wordlessly sat down. "Would you like to have something to drink?" I asked her and hoped to hear something in response and not get a shake of a head.

Luckily, she nodded before replying, "Scotch. Neat."

I stared at her for a moment because I knew how much she hated alcohol. My assistant saved me by sending one of the workers to fetch the drink and I started,

"I hope you have had the time to take a look at the proposal I have mailed you,"

"Yes. Everything was perfect," she answered, her eyes focused on the wood of the table. Her voice was lifeless just like the rest of her. It was as if instead of talking to Ruth Diaz I knew, I was talking to a ghost put in her body.

My assistant poured Ruth a glass of scotch and set it in front of her. Ruth immediately grabbed the glass and drowned its contents in a single go.

I gulped, my concern growing with the moment. Drake gave me a look before refilling her glass and fortunately, this time, she didn't drink it immediately.

"Can we just sign the contracts and be over with it," my heart shattered at her words, her eagerness to leave the room.

Her company had been facing breaches, and she had to find a new cybersecurity agency, so, she had turned to me for help.

She hadn't reached out by herself, of course. One of her employees had mailed my office and had asked us to send an offer.

I hadn't expected her to contact me ever again, but I would be lying if I were to say that I wasn't overjoyed to have at least some sort of connection with her.

Even if it was only on paper.

I had sent her a price that would give me a loss, but I just didn't want to lose the one opportunity I had to interact with her.

I gave her the papers that were already signed by me and her eyes didn't even skim over the details. I could've asked her to give me her entire company and she wouldn't have known.

She didn't care, and Ruth Diaz always cared about business.

She pulled out a pen from her purse, opened the cap, and directly went to sign the papers.

The nib of her pen touched the paper and she paused. "Do you always charge your customers so little?"

She gave me a sharp look, but this one wasn't demanding submission like before, this one wanted the truth. "You already have a running deal with Dante, so, we give you a discount if you take both the deals," I lied.

Ruth didn't buy it but she didn't pull out her gun and shoot me. She simply signed the papers and handed them back to me. She drowned the glass of scotch before rising to her feet.

She was about to leave when footsteps started approaching us. "That's Dante," I told her, assuming that she would want to meet her brother before leaving but instead, her eyes widened in fear: the first human emotion she'd shown in the entire day.

She gulped but didn't try to run since she knew it would be futile. It was either walking out the entrance: the same one from which Dante was about to enter, or she could climb down the fire exit in the snowstorm.

I wasn't entirely sure as to why she was avoiding Dante since the two of them were always nice to each other.

The door to my office opened and Dante entered but he wasn't alone like I had originally assumed.

He was with Kai, one of our potential clients, no doubt talking about the deal.

Dante stopped whatever he was saying the second he saw Ruth, but Ruth wasn't looking at him. Her eyes were on Kai.

Kai noticed her and unlike Dante, he smiled at her before walking towards her. "Hey, darling," he greeted her before pulling her in an embrace.

Ruth returned it, but her movements were forced at best. "Hi," her voice came out weaker than I had ever heard it.

I could see her shake from the inside. I would've been jealous, but the way her skin had paled at his sight, made me furious.

I was about to rip out Kai's arms when Ruth gently pulled away. Kai's one hand remained on her waist while the other tucked a loose strand of hair behind Ruth's ear.

He leaned forward and whispered something in Ruth's ear and let the hand on her waist slide lower. I rose from my seat, about to punch him in the face for groping her that way when he finally pulled away his hands.

"So glad to see you here, Ruth," he spoke, but his voice was dripping with malice that was meant only for Ruth. He turned to me and offered me a grin before greeting me, "Christian, I see you've met my fiancée,"

I froze. What the hell did he mean by fiancée?

The look on my face seemed to please him and his grin widened, "Ruth, haven't you told him about it?"

Ruth slowly shook her head and Kai reached out for her hand. She winced slightly as he touched her, but he made no move to console her. He merely raised her finger which had one of the biggest diamonds I had ever seen shining on it.

I turned to face Dante, about to ask him with my eyes why the hell had he approved their marriage but with the way his jaw had clenched, I realized that he had no clue about it either.

Ruth swiftly slid her hand out of his grip and Kai declared like he was a king, "Well, I'll take a leave now," but instead of leaving immediately, he pressed a kiss on Ruth's cheek before smirking in my direction and making his "grand" exist.

If I hadn't been entirely sure that Ruth hated him, I would've put a bullet through his head on the spot.

"What the hell, Ruth?" Dante snapped the second Kai was out of earshot.

"What do you mean?" Ruth asked, her face blank.

"You know damn well what I mean. Aren't you a little too old to go through a rebellious phase?" he yelled, making Ruth turn her head sharply in his direction. "So, I get pissed at you for whoring around and you find yourself a husband?"

"It was a business deal. It benefits both of our companies." Ruth replied crisply and in a manner that suggested that she had by-hearted the words.

Dante scoffed, "Oh please, you're trying to get me to apologize. Don't tell me this wasn't all preplanned. You just didn't *happen* to be here!"

The look on Ruth's face was of pure hurt, but instead of gracing him with a response, she grabbed a coat and made an exit that I would've been proud of had she not been on the verge of tears.

"Why the fuck would you say that, Dante?" I snapped. I had never been an aggressive person, but the way he had communicated with Ruth...it had made my blood boil.

I didn't know that they weren't on speaking terms anymore, but even if they weren't talking, he had no right to slut-shame her, especially after she'd confessed to me that she hadn't been intimate with a man for five and a half years before Alejandro.

"I fought with her for what she did to you!" came Dante's response. Memories of that afternoon often played in my head at nights, and I couldn't help but recount every single detail every time I thought of it, but the hickeys hurt the most.

The mark of someone else on her. Someone else's claim on her. It was enough to unravel me.

When I had gone to visit my sister, she'd told me that I had fallen in love. Of course, she had quickly amended that statement and had concluded that I was on my way to that.

I was about to fall in love with her. As in moments away.

I had driven back as fast as I could and had gotten back to following Ruth. Alex didn't deserve her, especially after he'd left her in the middle of the road and had gone to have dinner like it was not a big deal.

I was so certain that I was going to woo her back and that I would wait for her, but the second she'd come to me, I had pushed her away, solely because I thought it wasn't love.

I thought maybe, if I would give it some time, it would all fade away, that it wasn't love because how could it be love when I felt something for another woman and she felt something for another man?

But over the last three months, it had only gotten worse. I missed her when I was alone, I missed her when I was with people and I spent an unhealthy amount of time imagining conversations with her to an extent that I felt absolutely fucked in the head.

I had been a mess, and I didn't mean to be over-presumptuous, but by the look on her face, she had been a mess as well, but her mess was of a different kind.

It was as if someone, *I*, had taken out everything that made her who she was and had killed it.

The only satisfying work that I had done in the past three months was to make her ex-husband's life hell in prison.

On my way back from my sister's house, I had looked a little into her relationship with her husband. I hadn't read it all: I wanted her to open up to me, but the consistent physical abuse had been enough to make me want to kill him.

I couldn't do that. He was Leah's biological father and Ruth once loved him.

However, what I could do was use some of my less-than-moral contacts to harass her husband while he was in jail.

I wanted him to know how it felt to be helpless when people beat the shit out of you, just like he had done with Ruth.

The only difference was that Ruth could've fought back. Ryan wasn't exactly muscular: he had more of a lean build, and Ruth had been trained for years. She could've killed him for laying a hand on her. As much as I didn't understand why she hadn't killed him, the point was that Ryan couldn't fight back, and that was the worst thing for a man's ego.

But my ego had died the second Ruth had walked inside the room. It was replaced by anger that had only intensified when Dante had insulted Ruth.

And now, he blamed me. Bastard.

"What the fuck are you talking about?" I asked him, my voice sounding like a snarl to my own ears.

"She cheated on you," Four words that would've torn me apart had they been true.

"She did no such thing. She made it clear that we weren't a thing long ago. Plus, if anyone cheated, it was me," I admitted. Ruth had slept with Alex once. I had spent months fucking Julia. I was a bitch for being such a sore player.

"What the fuck do you mean?"

"I dated Julia. Ruth started dating Alejandro when I was with Julia. She wasn't at fault,"

Dante's eyes widened as the realization sunk in and he pressed a fist to his mouth. But Dante's tantrums weren't significant at that moment.

What was important was how Ruth had acted around her *fiancé*, again, a man I would prefer dead.

She didn't want him near her, much less pulling her into hugs and groping her in front of her brother. I could see how much she disliked him in her eyes.

Ruth had no reason to marry for business. She had all the wealth in the world, and every magazine had labeled her as one of the richest women on the earth.

Kai was just a millionaire. Sure, he had the looks, had the power, but he had no charisma.

He was an asshole who had almost been jailed five times for sexual assault.

Plus, his chain of stores was densely concentrated around Ruthless's stores, which reduced the profit Ruth could've gained from anyone else.

She could've married a Russian, a French, an Italian: all of them would've actually made her good enough profit for her to sacrifice her life.

But why would she marry a man who she neither loved nor needed?

Only one reason.

Ruth was being blackmailed.

11

Ruth

Emily had transitioned from being my assistant to being my nurse. Instead of having to spend her time answering my emails, she had to spend her time applying ointment to my wounds.

Kai had a habit...a habit that defined him in my mind. He wasn't a sweet fiancé in my head. He was an abusive soon-to-be husband who I couldn't kill.

Kai had his men hack into my system, and at that very moment, he had all my bank statements and account details, and his men ready to destroy my apps and websites from within.

He had given me a choice to either marry him or let my company collapse.

I had chosen the former, despite how it came with many issues like giving him thirty percent of the shares and displaying my clothes at his stores.

It also came with me being his punching bag, but that was tolerable. I was used to having an abusive husband, what I wasn't used to was not having control.

I had to agree to everything that he said, had to do everything he asked me to do and I absolutely hated it.

It wasn't normal for me to listen to a man, much less let him dictate my life but there wasn't much that I could do.

Talking back was five lashes. Disobeying him was ten. And his bad moods equaled as many lashes as he liked.

My back had scars overlapping each other. Some portions of my skin had stopped healing from the repeated whipping, while the rest were taking excruciatingly long.

Emily cleaned my wounds after every whipping. She didn't ask questions because she didn't have to. She was my assistant and the one person who had to know about the situation so she could help me handle it.

After cleaning my wounds for the hundredth time, she bandaged my back and helped me rise. In a way, the beatings had started to hurt less, but after he was done, they hurt a lot more. The whip was starting to cut to the bone, and he was starting to enjoy it less and less, making him invent new ways of hurting me.

Knives were his new fascinating. Originally, he had turned to different kinds of whips, but with every week, he changed his weapon, to a point where he ran out of good whips and moved to using knives after he was done giving me his regular round of whipping.

I had a hundred cuts on my back. Some were random, some were drawings, and some were words. There was a rose drawn next to a heart. There were stars and a moon and a sun. There was 'slut' written in bold letters and 'whore' written in beautiful calligraphy from the time that I had worn something that showed my cleavage.

He was a psychopath, blaming me for my 'disobedience'. He was one of those men who liked power and respect but when people refused to give them that, they resorted to being cruel and forcing their hand.

He was just a man seeking for domination.

Kai was nowhere close to being unattractive: he had a muscular build, beautiful dark hair, and deep blue eyes that attracted every girl's attention. But most girls were smart: they sensed the evil in him right away and kept their distance and that was what irked Kai.

No girl would listen to him willingly, so he forced them the same way he was forcing me.

I had a plan, of course, I did. I just had to pull off the wedding till I was done signing my security services' responsibility to Christian and then wait for him to remove the bugs in my system.

The plan was going considerably well and discreetly until Kai found me in Christian's office.

He thought we were fucking, which was better in a way, but it certainly felt like hell when his whips were cutting my bone and the blade of his knife was an inch deep in my back.

But the pain was good. It helped me forget about the reality. The world where the love of my life hated me and my brother thought of me as a slut just like the rest of my family. The world where my heart wasn't literally collapsing.

Emily handed me a glass of water and I gulped down my medicines. They were to be taken after having food, but I couldn't find it in myself to choke down anything.

Ever since my heart attack three months ago, I had to start taking my medicines regularly. I was lucky to have survived without any medical aid but you only got lucky once.

I had no wish to push that luck, so after an echo and an ECG, my cardiologist had prescribed me some medicines and I took them every day.

My health had only gotten worse with the continuous blood loss and it was straining my heart.

But I couldn't tell Kai, he could never know that there was something that could destroy me so easily.

Emily was about to scold me for skipping dinner when the doorbell rang.

I jumped to my feet. I wasn't expecting anyone. Hazel was the only friend I had and my clients never visited. It could be Dante in case he wanted to apologize, or...

My heart started beating in an unnatural rhythm and Emily went to check out the mysterious person.

It took her a few minutes, and when she returned alone, disappointment crawled in my head.

She was holding a bag that had the logo of a nearby restaurant and I asked her, "Did you order it?"

She shook her head before handing me the bag. I opened it to find boxes filled with food and a note that had a single word and a punctuation.

Eat. It read.

My heart's beating got rapid back again as I realized there was only one person who could send me that.

Biting my lip, I pulled out the contents of the bag and began eating, happy that our little routine had restarted.

Right when I was done, an email notification popped up on my phone. I clicked on it to find a message from an anonymous, probably spam email address, but I opened it because very few people had that email address of mine.

The email had no subject and two lines in the body:

Kai no longer has something against you.

You are free.

I paused mid-bite. There were only two people who could've pulled it off and one of them had no clue about the situation.

Christian had my company's security for less than six hours and he had managed to push all Kai's hackers out of the system.

And it only meant one thing.

I dialled Kreg, the head of my physical security. "Get Kai and save him for me,"

Emily gave me a wary look but she didn't say a word. She knew what I was going to do and she knew that Kai had it coming.

When I got to the warehouse, Kreg had a set of weapons ready in front of Kai for me to use, but I didn't have to use them.

I pulled out the papers and slid them towards him with a pen.

He was tied up to a chair, bleeding from his head, but he still managed to lean forward and read them.

"No," was all that escaped his mouth after he took one look at the papers.

I smirked. "You don't have a choice, Kai. I have people who could kill you right now with impunity. No one would even find your body.

However, if you sign these documents, I might consider letting you live,"

Power. Kai wanted power. And he had lost it.

My smile darkened as Kreg cut his right hand loose and Kai signed the documents that transferred all his shares of his own company 'Marble' to me.

"If I even get the hint that you are considering taking this matter to the court, I will kill you. Without hesitation," I added.

Kai saw the reality of the threat in my eyes and shrunk back in fear.

"Throw him on the roads in some remote area. Make sure he stays alive,"

I could've killed him, but taking away his power was way more satisfying.

Realizing that I owed someone a 'thank you', the next person I went to visit was Christian Walker, but I didn't forget to pick up a gift on my way.

Christian probably didn't even remember, but we had met over a decade ago before meeting at my office.

He was young and had gotten himself in trouble, and I was there for an important mission. His parents were rich, so I had never understood why they had chosen such a shabby neighborhood that was filled with criminals, but curiosity was pushed to the back of my mind when Christian had asked me to go home for my own safety when he was bleeding to his death in a place where no one else would save him.

I had two guns and three knives. I could've taken down a dozen armed men with that, so naturally, I stayed.

I stayed until the paramedics arrived and then I disappeared like a shadow.

Perhaps Christian hadn't remembered my face because of how traumatic that night had been for him, but I had never been able to forget his.

I found myself wondering, night after night, how someone could be so selfless, especially when they were dealing with strangers.

It made no sense to sense to me because everyone in my life at that time had been selfish. My parents only cared about their image and looks, my boyfriend about himself, and Dante was in college two states away.

I had no one who cared for me selflessly apart from Dante and Alex for a long time. So, when I saw Christian again, I didn't wait before asking him out.

My mistake was being a bitch, but I wasn't letting him get away. Love or not, I cared for him. I cared for him enough to want to give it a shot no matter how badly it had ended the last time.

I parked the car in the third basement after getting my gate clearance. The receptionist gave me a lift pass, and a few minutes later, I was standing in front of his door with two roses in my hands.

One was the one I had retrieved the day after he had dropped it in front of my door. It was dry and its petals were crushed.

The other one was a fresh new rose.

Christian opened the door in record time as if he was expecting me, and the fact that he knew I would come for him touched me.

He was in a suit that was the exact color of his eyes. His looked perfect, the way one usually did at their own wedding. Damn, I would've definitely married him at that moment had he asked me to.

The fresh rose was behind my back and I reached out to give him the crinkled rose and said, "You left this at my place,"

His gave darkened but instead of reaching for the rose, he grabbed my hips and pulled me towards him. I gasped, and instead of letting go of me, he used his other hand to retrieve the rose behind my back.

"There's a CCTV to your right," he whispered, his voice deep and rough and I turned my head to find it, but before I could find it, he grabbed my chin and swirled my head gently to look at him.

I was inches from his face when he brought the rose close to his nose, right between our faces, and he inhaled.

The action caused me to tip my head forward, and in an attempt to cover up my urge to kiss him, I inhaled deeply as well.

That seemed to break his restraint because he closed the gap between us and crushed his lips on mine.

12

Christian

———◦♡◦———

I pulled Ruth inside and closed the door. I briefly pulled away from the kiss to look at her, but she didn't let me pause.

She grabbed my neck and pulled me in for another kiss. The roses in our hands fell to the floor as we reached out to touch each other more.

My hand on her waist slid upward, making her wince.

I immediately paused and pulled back to look at her in the eyes. Her gaze went to the floor, and I realized that something was wrong.

"Turn around," I ordered as softly as I could, and she obeyed without any complaint.

I rolled her top upwards slowly, trying not to be inappropriate. She didn't ask me to stop, so, I took it as a green signal to raise it until I saw her skin, but I found none.

Her back was covered entirely in bandages and gauzes and some of them were already soaking with blood. "Who did this?" I asked her, my voice calm, unlike how I felt on the inside.

"Kai," she answered, her voice breathless despite how unexerted she remained.

"Get on the bed," I ordered, just as gently as the last time and she didn't argue yet again. I didn't have to ask her, she herself removed her top.

Her back was entirely covered with bandages, and some gauze pads extended to her front as well for support.

She was in a dark brown bra, and I had to try really hard to not ask her why her lingerie was colorful, unlike her external clothes.

"Can I clean it up?" I asked genuinely. Given the recent incidents, I wasn't sure whether she was comfortable being touched around her scars, especially by a man, and I wanted to be sure.

She nodded and lied face-first on the mattress. I grabbed my kit, which had a lot more than just first aid, and I cut open her earlier bandages until she was in nothing but her bra.

"The blood will ruin your sheets," she warned me, making me kneel down and press a small kiss on her neck in response.

I unclasped her bra but didn't take it off. It wasn't necessary to clean up her scars, and I knew she was in no condition to go on any other road.

Her back looked awful: it was covered completely by blood and wounds, leaving very little skin unharmed. I had the sudden urge to tear Kai apart limb by limb until he was nothing but a withering piece of meat begging to be free.

I began cleaning her wounds. At first, she didn't give any reaction, but after a few moments, I saw her grip tighten on the sheets, clearly showing how much it was hurting her.

"I'll kill him," I vowed to make her feel a little better and I was completely honest. I was going to kill him.

"Don't," she replied, her voice low, perhaps from the pain that she was desperately trying to hide.

I didn't ask for her reasons because I knew that if she was letting him live, she had a reason behind it. Instead, I kept on working on her back, bandaging up her wounds after I was done.

"The bra would hurt," I told her, trying not to sound like a creep. She nodded, and I pulled out a tee shirt of mine and offered it to her.

It was grey with black writings, and I could only hope that it was black enough for her.

She pressed a hand to her chest to keep her bra from falling off while she used another hand to take the tee from my hands.

She pulled it over her head before removing her bra straps from her arms and pulling out the bra and setting it on my bedside table.

I cupped her cheeks and helped her get to her feet. "Leah must be waiting for you,"

She didn't deny it and I knew for a fact that I was right. She could probably be asleep, but children missed their parents the most at night, especially when their parents were working during the day.

Ruth let the rest of her clothes be as I walked her to the door and then out to where her car was in the basement. She let me drive to her house, where we continued right where we had left off before I had discovered her injuries because Leah was fast asleep by the time we had reached home.

I didn't let go far because of how bad her wounds were, but we spent a significant amount of time just making out, making up for all those months during which we should've been together but we weren't.

Ruth's lips were swollen and she was half asleep when I decided to let her sleep.

I lied back down on her bed and pulled on top of me, to not let her back bear the weight of her body as I gripped her shoulders tightly and held her firmly to her side.

It only took her minutes to fall asleep, but it took me hours to get over the way she looked when she was at peace, and her face was shining under the moonlight, making her look literally like a goddess.

When I woke up the next day, Ruth was already out of bed. I rose and grabbed my shirt from the floor that we had taken off during our intense make-out session.

I found her in the kitchen making something on the stove. Her hair was wet, and she looked like she had showered, but for some reason, she was still in my tee shirt.

"What are you making?" I asked her as I approached her from behind. I slid my arms around her waist, hugging her from behind and peeping over her shoulder to see what she was cooking.

"Pasta," she replied. "I owe you some," she added, referring to the time when I had made her pasta on her period.

I kissed her cheek and she smiled up at me.

I let her finish while I looked around the kitchen for a coffee maker and made myself some coffee. "You want some?" I asked her and she shook her head in response.

It was a school day, so, Leah was already awake and was running around behind Albert, trying to find a notebook.

In front of the six feet man, she looked like a puppy, running around between his legs. It was only after she had found her book, that she noticed me.

"Christian!" she squealed before running towards me. I pulled her in my arms and picked her up.

"Hey champ!" she giggled at the nickname before grabbing my face and kissing my cheek. I raised an eyebrow at Ruth out of amusement and Ruth pulled Leah out of my arms and set on the floor.

"But, mom-"

"You have school, darling. You can play with Christian after you come back," she told Leah gently. Leah pouted but agreed nonetheless.

She bid the two of us goodbye as Albert escorted her outside.

"I am so sorry about that," Ruth apologized, burying her face in her hands.

"Don't worry about it, cat, she's just a kid!" I told her honestly.

"Cat?"

"Yes, you're just like a cute little black cat. You think you're so scary and dangerous and everyone else thinks that of you too, but for me, you are a harmless little cutie pie,"

Ruth flushed, and I kissed her, unable to resist the blush around her cheeks.

"But I think 'diamond' suits you more. You do have a net worth that high. Plus, you are just as beautiful, definitely just as hard to get,"

She chuckled before turning the stove off. "A bit of a warning: I can't cook!"

I wasn't sure whether we were official or not, but if by any chance we were since the night before, then our relationship would've been the shortest one in the history had I not dodged it by drowning the first bite with a huge gulp of water.

Salty was an understatement for how the pasta tasted, and the high amount of oregano made me realize how serious she was when she'd told me that she couldn't cook.

Damn, she wasn't kidding.

Luckily, Ruth didn't notice it, and I continued eating it like it was the best thing I had ever had, complimenting her here and there.

I hated how her smile vanished when she herself tried the dish. She started coughing and I handed her a glass of water to help her out.

"You told me it was delicious!" she complained, drinking every last drop.

"I didn't want to hurt you," I confessed.

She kissed me slowly and both of us jerked back from the lingering taste of salt on both of our lips.

Just as the laughter died, I remembered that we needed to have an important conversation.

I tucked a strand of her hair behind her ear, and started, "I am sorry,"

Her smile didn't waver as she answered, "It's okay. And, I am sorry as well,"

"It wasn't your fault, Ruth. I was the one who started going out with Julia when you were in Paris and there's no excuse. Even after everything, I thought that if we weren't sure about each other, then there was no point. But the last three months have been hell for me. And seeing you like this, knowing that none of this would've happened if I wouldn't have left you, it hurt. I know no apology would ever-"

"Stop. Don't apologize for things you didn't do! It. Wasn't. Your. Fault. Period. Now, don't aggravate me by saying anything or I'll bite you!" she threatened playfully, mimicking a cat bite that didn't fail to make me laugh.

I kissed her again and she wrapped her around me after we pulled back. "I am just glad things got here,"

I got to work a little late, and Dante figured out where I had been. I was pissed as hell at the guy, but I knew he hated himself more, so, I didn't push it.

He didn't say anything at first, but after we finished off an important meeting, he approached me. "You have no idea how ashamed I am,"

I did. I knew exactly how ashamed her was but I didn't say anything.

"Is she okay?"

"Her entire back is covered with wounds. I forced her to go to an orthopaedic today to get her vertebrae checked out. The marks looked like the whips had cut through the skin. They'll take months to heal, but she'll be fine,"

Dante closed his eyes in agony before letting his head fall in his hands.

"I fucked up,"

"Yes,"

"Will you take me to her? I need to apologize," he asked me hopefully and I nodded.

"But say one wrong thing..." I trailed off in a warning and Dante nodded solemnly.

We picked out some Mexican food on our way to Ruth's house after we were done with our work. It was time for dinner, and Dante had assumed that showing up with food would help his case.

I let them stand in front of me as he knocked on the front door. We heard a few giggles come from the other side, belonging to three different people.

Two of them were Ruth and Leah. The third one' voice felt familiar but I couldn't exactly pinpoint who it was.

Dante froze at the sound, but before he could hide like he looked like he wanted to, the door opened.

13

Ruth

I followed Hazel as she rushed to open the door. We both knew Christian would be coming over, and Hazel was so enamored by his stories that I'd asked her that she had stayed behind to meet him.

Until the knock had come, it was just us three girls fangirling over Christian together.

After that, it was a long stretch of awkward silence as Hazel took in the form of Dante.

My eyes met with Dante's and I looked away, the pain of the previous day cutting me all over again.

Christian shot me an apologetic glance, but I didn't let my gaze linger on him either. "What do you want?" I asked Dante, whose eyes didn't move from Hazel even after my question. "Dante?" I snapped my fingers to get his attention and it seemed to work.

He turned towards me and cleared his throat. "I wanted to apologize to you. Can I come in?"

I didn't reply, but pushed the door open wider. Dante took a tentative step in and Christian followed him.

Dante didn't take his eyes off Hazel as he walked in, despite the fact that Hazel's gaze remained elsewhere.

He held out a bag of food in my directions and Christian helped me set the dinner. I wanted to open the cabinet to my right and smash all the crockery on the floor to get some sort of release, but Leah was still in the room, and I didn't want her to see that side of me.

Dante continued staring at Hazel for a better part of the dinner, not bothering to say anything to me. My brother wasn't such an asshole most of the time, but if it was about Hazel, then he gladly tuned out everyone else including me.

Hazel had been my best friend since I was sixteen, and that was exactly how long she and Dante had known each other.

Honestly? Dante had a thing for her since the moment she walked into his life.

She was seeing someone else at that time and Dante had just broken up with his girlfriend. Their story was as complicated as it was tragic. Now, years later, Dante had found someone else. Hazel hadn't.

She never bitched about my brother in front of me but I knew the extent of how much he'd hurt her over the years.

I had gotten involved, had tried to help them sort it out, but it had never worked.

And now, I could see the remorse in Dante's eyes as he tried to find something in Hazel's ones filled with pain.

My brother had managed to transform one of the most loving and cheerful girls into a person who rarely smiled, much less cared for anyone in general.

The dinner passed awkwardly, and Hazel was the first one to get up. Dante didn't try to stop her, but he didn't leave her be either.

It was a routine of theirs: whenever Hazel left alone, Dante followed her home with his car and made sure that she got home safely.

After they both left, I tucked in Leah and then, Christian offered to change my bandages.

The bleeding hadn't stopped completely, and I knew some places needed stitches, so, I had asked a doctor to take a look at my wounds that afternoon, so, I had to decline Christian's offer.

He assumed it was because I was mad, and honestly, I was a little pissed. I wasn't going to lie and say that I was fine.

"I am so sorry, I just…" his voice trailed off. He didn't have to explain it. I knew why he had done it, and it made sense.

"I am not mad about it, Christian, it's just that you could've told me," He nodded and his gaze fell to the floor in shame. "Don't feel so bad. I just wish I could've gotten Hazel out."

"What's up with those two?" he asked. "I thought they loved each other,"

"They did. Once. I think they still do, but there's just so much past between the two of them…"

I let my head fall against Christian's chest and he pulled me closer.

Everything had happened so fast, and I still hadn't digested it all.

He probably sensed the exhaustion coming from me because he slowly picked me up and walked me to my bedroom.

He laid me down gently on my bed and grabbed me my pyjamas from my wardrobe.

The wardrobe in my cupboard mostly consisted of relaxing outfits. My closet, however, was filled with my dresses and suits and everything a girl could ever dream of.

I changed in my nightwear on the bed and he pulled a blanket over me before asking softly, "How's your back?"

"It's...fine. Hurts less than yesterday,"

He grabbed my face and tenderly kissed my forehead before pulling away. "I'll go to the guest room,"

"No!" I complained instantly, grabbing his arms before he could walk away. "Stay..." I muttered childishly, making him grin.

"Sometimes I forget how young you are," he joked and I shot him a glare but pulled him down beside me nonetheless.

He stroked my hair until I fell asleep.

But he didn't know that my sound sleep was going to be dismantled so soon. I shot straight up as the ringing of my phone pierced the quiet of the night.

Very few people had my number, and if someone was calling so late, it was probably because it was an emergency.

It was Hazel. I quickly picked up the call and answered it just as Christian stirred awake beside me.

"What happened?" I asked her.

"Ruth..." she started, her voice inconsistent. "I...You're...thank you so much for being my friend, Ruth..." she didn't sound drunk. She sounded like she was out of breath and exhausted and half dead. "I love you, girl...Tell Dante, I..."

Her voice broke off and I heard the sound of the phone clattering to the ground. "Hazel!" I called out, the panic slowly getting me. "Hazel!" I screamed and Christian jumped to his feet,

"What happened?"

My chest felt too tight like suddenly the air in my lungs had been filled with water, but I managed to stop myself from hyperventilating.

I had to help her. I could panic later.

I called the police and an ambulance and asked them to get to her place. Christian overheard that, and quickly grabbed a sleeping Leah and a tee shirt for me while my driver pulled out my car.

Luckily, I was on Hazel's list of emergency numbers, so I received a call from the hospital they admitted her into. The bad thing was that there was someone else on the list.

My brother.

He had gotten sooner probably cause we had to drop off Leah at Bianca's place. He was sitting in the waiting area with his head in his hands, his form motionless, as he waited.

I had talked to a doctor, and had found out about the cause of the accident.

Hazel had slit her wrists and would've died if the paramedics hadn't gotten there when they had.

She wouldn't have survived at all.

But even now, she was in coma. The doctors weren't sure whether she was going to make it or not, and had asked us to give it a day.

The major blood loss had caused her brain to shut down and she was on a ventilator while the doctors did the best they could. Dante had already called the best people he knew, and I had scoured my contacts and had called a former friend to help me out with the situation.

But his assistant had received the call and had informed me that he was going to be in a surgery for the next four hours and had three surgeries scheduled right after that one.

There was no way he would ever make it in time and I was forced to sit and wait while the other doctors worked on Hazel.

I had never been more grateful to have Christian by my side. While I refused to make conversation with Dante, Christian kept me distracted as much as he could by telling me about his sisters, his family, his childhood stories.

When nothing worked, he pulled me into his lap and stroked my hair until I fell asleep.

Dante was still awake and in the same position when I woke up. He was staring straight ahead, his eyes glassy and zoned out, and the only emotion evident was given by the way he moved his fingers across the chair.

Christian made me sit while he brough coffee and food for us from the vending machine. I managed to chug down the coffee, even though the food remained hard to swallow.

Dante didn't move, didn't respond to Christian's request, just continued staring straight ahead blankly.

I took the coffee from Christian's hands and sat quietly beside Dante. I wrapped an arm around his shoulder and rubbed his arm gently, slowly trying to bring him back to reality.

He didn't jerk awake like I had expected him to. He tenderly put an arm on my back and pulled me closer, making me bite my lower lip in pain.

He noticed and cursed under his breath before grabbing my head and kissing my temple gently. "I am sorry," he whispered, his voice hollow.

"It's okay," I didn't hold anything against him. He had done enough for me over the years to make me forgive him for anything and everything.

I brought the coffee to his lips and he took a small sip of it before jerking back, clutching his chest.

Reflux, I realized. I rubbed his back before holding out some water for him to drink first. He took his time emptying the bottle and when I offered him coffee again, he shook his head.

He laid his head down on my lap and plopped his feat on the chairs beside his, half-stretching them. "Do you want to sleep properly?" I asked him but he declined.

"I want to be here when she wakes up. Which she will,"

His words were confident, but hope was seeping out of every word that left his mouth. He was reassuring himself, telling himself that she'd be fine, that the love of his life would survive, even though she probably wouldn't.

"I told her I loved her, Ruth," he confessed out of nowhere, his voice cracking. "Why would she do this after hearing that?"

Suddenly, I remembered Hazel's request to deliver to a message to Dante. "When she called me earlier today...she asked me to tell you that she loved you,"

That had to be what she wanted to tell him. What else could be there?

Dante's head snapped to face mine and I saw tears in my brother's eyes after years. "Tell me she'll be alright,"

I bent down and kissed his forehead. "She'll be fine," I tried my best to keep my voice from breaking apart and from the lies to escape from the sentence.

Half of the ventilated patients didn't survive. The hours passing by were crucial: every single minute was. I suddenly regretted the coffee that I had had as it rose in my throat.

I managed to smile as Dante looked at me for comfort and made it look like it was all going to be fine.

But it wasn't.

Dante had a girlfriend waiting for him at his home when he'd told another girl that he loved her and it had messed up with the girl so badly that she'd tried to kill herself.

Dante had to choose. Hazel had to choose. They were killing each other, quite literally so from the looks of it.

But I would pay for the painful drama to unfold as long as Hazel was going to be alive for it.

There was nothing I wanted more.

Christian and I weren't dating officially, but he still didn't leave out any efforts to help me or Dante out.

He slept even less than I did. He kept on getting us coffees, food (and not just packets from the vending machine), and forced us to take showers in the hospital's bathrooms in the VIP waiting rooms, where they had shifted us to in the afternoon.

Much to his disdain, he had to leave me and Dante alone, but only because he had to look after Dante's workload as well.

Dante didn't even have the strength to offer to go to the office, and he was as much of a workaholic as I was, if not more.

Dante only skipped work due to emergencies, which were very rare in his life, because his criteria for something to count as an emergency was unbelievable.

My mom's appendix removal surgery wasn't an emergency. My dad getting hospitalized after an accident wasn't an emergency. Naomi fighting with a coworker was one. Me having pregnancy mood swings and craving icecream was one.

Honestly, to Dante, the emergencies were classified as so on the basis of who they concerned. If they concerned me or Naomi, then yes, they were definitely emergencies.

If they concerned our monsters of parents, then it could be their last moments and his work would still matter more.

That's how messed up his system was.

And I was well aware of it. Dante didn't care for too many people, only those who cared back for him. He was kind to me, and for me, he would always be a loving older brother, but from how he was with Hazel, I knew for a fact that he had a darker side.

Hazel never told me everything that went down between the two of them. She respected the dilemma I would be in if I had to choose between the two of them, and so, kept it to herself.

She never told me anything, and I could never bring myself to ask.

The brother in my mind had to be real. He could not be just an imaginative figure who went around ruining people at his wish.

But Dante was a dangerous man. He dabbled in underground works just enough to secure his power, but even the tiniest toe in the water was dangerous.

I stayed miles away from that area cause I had a daughter to look after, but Dante had no one but me and Leah to lose, and the connection between us was severed enough to keep us safe.

Plus, in his mind, if something were to happen to him, Leah and I would survive. Emotional distress aside, we would be fine.

He loved Hazel, enough to kill people, kill himself for her, but not enough to want to live for her, not enough to want less power and more safety.

But at that moment, I could see Dante regret everything wrong he'd done. He blamed himself, perhaps believing that it was karma coming for him.

The question ringing in my mind was: why?

Why would Hazel suicide?

She had been fine in front of me mere hours back. Sure, she had met Dante, and it could've dampened her mood but of course it wasn't enough to make her want to kill herself.

But Dante had followed her home. I knew that they'd talked and they'd gotten into a huge fight. That would explain why Dante looked so guilty.

I had to know the reason. Was it because Dante had confessed his love for her or was it something else?

But I couldn't bring myself to ask him. I would rather have some tucked away resentment against him in the corner of my brain about my best friend *probably* suiciding cause of him than knowing for sure that he'd been the reason.

Yes, I could live with the former, but the later would kill me.

14

Christian

—♡—

I signed some papers on behalf of Dante and finished my work as soon as I could so I could get back to Ruth.

Ruth really seemed to care about Hazel, because for the first few hours while we waited in the hospital, she'd looked worse than I had ever seen her.

And Dante looked even worse. I knew he loved Hazel, and losing, or even the fear of losing the woman you loved was pain worse than anything.

Maybe I hadn't loved Ruth back then, but for the moments during which I had feared that she'd die, I had lost it.

Even Kai laying a hand on her had driven me to the brink of insanity, and in those moments of madness, I had contacted a criminal and had asked him for his help.

Alejandro da Silva was the most infamous hacker, and doing what needed to be done required a particular set of skills I didn't have.

He'd helped me get through that portion, and had even offered to take the first flight there and kill Kai with his bare hands for touching Ruth, but I denied simply to give Ruth the pleasure of doing so.

She'd been kind enough to let him live, but I hadn't been so kind.

I had tracked him down and had gotten all his assets seized or frozen by anonymously releasing statements relating to tax evasion and his involvement in criminal activities.

I hadn't killed him, I wasn't a psycho. Plus, killing would be too simple. Too short of a process.

I wanted him to suffer like Ruth had, to watch his empire slip from under him and be able to do nothing about it.

Ruth was too kind, but when it came to her, I was anything but that.

I hated myself for not knowing about it sooner, but now that I had her security under me, I could very well do and see through everything. No one would ever be able to threaten her again, much less hurt her.

Even if it was death.

If Ruth wanted Hazel alive, Hazel would live.

I would make sure of that.

I had already called the best doctors from all over the world since Dante's reach was limited to the country.

They had all abandoned their work and had flown over to look over Hazel. They were doing their best, and things were looking better.

The survival rate was low, but she would make it. Three of those doctors had sworn it with their lives even though it went against their morals. Probably cause they would hate to anger a billionaire and two millionaires involved with E.Y.E.

Apparently, they weren't just giving false reassurances. By the time I got back, Hazel had gotten out of the coma. She was still knocked out, but she was out of danger.

Ruth finally looked a little better and Dante had fallen asleep in her lap. She had a hand on his head, stroking his hair slowly, softly, as he quietly laid there.

I gently lifted his head off her lap, and Ruth opened her mouth in complaint but I caught her words with my lips as I captured her mouth in a kiss and put Dante's head on a pillow.

"Christian-" Ruth started, but I pulled away and cut her off,

"You need to get your bandages changed," was all I said before taking her into my arms. I made no effort to make her get to her feet despite my words. I pressed my face into the neck before lowering her into my lap. "You want me to do it?" I asked her and she pressed a hand against my chest before whispering,

"Christian..."

My name on her tongue coming out as breathless as it did made me press her closer to me. It wasn't time. She was upset and hurt and I was just...

"You know I'll be gentle..."

She gave me a look that said that it wasn't about me being gentle. I sighed in defeat, making her take my face in her hand. "I am sorry-"

"Don't you dare apologize for this, Cat. I am sorry for being senseless enough to bring it up right now,"

"It's not your fault that I am irresistible,"

"Keep up that attitude and it'll be the only thing that you'll be keeping," I answered, my gaze lowering to her clothes suggestively.

She blushed so hard, her cheeks turned almost as red as the curtains covering the windows. I pecked her forehead before rising and pulling her to her feet and guiding her to a doctor I had asked for help.

They returned fifteen minutes later and at the same time Hazel's chief doctor came with the newest updates.

"Is she okay?" Ruth asked directly and the doctor replied,

"She's fine. She should be awake by tomorrow morning!"

Ruth let herself fall into my arms due from the sheer exhaustion and I held her firmly. I thanked the doctor before taking Ruth into my arms and walking her to her room in the hospital which was right beside Dante's.

I set her down as tenderly as I could without hurting her back and covered her with a blanket. She flipped herself on her front, probably to lessen the pain caused by the wounds on her back, and it made my throat dry all over again.

I let my fingers tangle her almost perfectly combed hair before letting them seep deeper and massage her scalp. I padded the soft skin gently with my fingers before reducing my touch to a ghost-like presence, tenderly stroking her scalp at places, making her hum in approval.

I smiled before leaning down and pressing a kiss against the back of her head.

She grabbed my hand and pressed it against her chest where I could hear her beating heart. She snuggled against it wordlessly, not having to explain her point.

She wanted to show me the kind of effect I had on her, and I suddenly had the urge to do the same: take her hand and show her what something as simple as hearing the beating of her heard did to me, but I resisted.

I gently retrieved my hand and grabbed another blanket. I opened it but not entirely. I spread it against the bed, and turned Ruth around on her back, hoping that the blanket would make her feel more comfortable.

She gave no complains, probably because she had fallen asleep by the time I was done.

A doctor came to visit us at four in the morning to inform us that Hazel had woken up. I was awake and working on a project, but Ruth looked so utterly exhausted that I couldn't bring myself to disturb her.

I told the doctor to wait till the morning and he raised no issues.

Ruth woke up earlier than I had expected. She rose in a perfectly mannered way not looking at all like she'd just woken up.

She could be on the cover of Barbie saying, 'I woke up like this' while pointing to her set hair and straight clothes.

It was probably cause she hadn't stirred at all in her sleep. She had slept in a certain way and had woken up just that way.

She looked over at me with no dizziness in her eyes. "Didn't you sleep at all last night?" she asked with a frown.

I shook my head in response and her eyes widened and she jumped to her feet.

"You need to sleep!"

"I have some work to take care of-" I started but stopped myself when I noticed the guilt on her face. "It's not your fault, Diamond,"

She sighed before replying, "I know, it's just that..." she trailed off before suddenly wrapping her arms around me. She was standing, and even though I was sitting, my head fell against her nape, despite the chair being too small. "What work do you have left?" she asked, without letting go of me.

"Some emails to answer to," I replied, pulling her closer to me by her shoulders.

She pulled back a little to look me in the eye. "Can I answer them?"

The sincerity in her eyes tugged at my heart, making me smile a little. "Hazel's awake, don't you want to see her first?"

She jumped with happiness, chuckling a little as she pulled me back into a hug, this time kissing my cheek as well.

"My lips feel betrayed," I complained jokingly. Her cheeks turned red as she pulled back and pressed a small kiss against my lips before pulling back. "Too short," I pouted and she laughed a little before grabbing my head and kissing me properly.

I kissed her back, satisfied completely by the exchange. Her friend was fine and she was happy. That was all I wanted.

Fifteen minutes later, she freshened up and we were walking to Hazel's room. There was security to make sure that she wasn't going to hurt herself again and a doctor was sitting with three nurses to see that she was fine.

Hazel was half sitting with her neck against the pillow. Her eyes looked tired, and she stared ahead with no emotions in them, and that remained unchanged even when she saw Ruth.

"What's wrong?" Ruth asked, her smile falling.

"Why did you do it?" Hazel questioned back, her voice hoarse. Ruth stared at her in confusion, making Hazel simplify her question, "Why did you save me?"

"What do you mean?"

"I made my choice. You had no right to save me!"

"Hazel-"

"Go away, Ruth, I don't want to see you right now,"

I had to witness Ruth's face drop and she left without any complaints or arguments. I followed her after throwing a glace Hazel's way. The girl looked too broken to even be sitting upright, and I felt as much concern for her at that moment as I felt for Ruth.

"You should sleep," Ruth suggested, trying to avoid the topic. She didn't want to talk about it and I respected that, so I didn't push her.

Instead, I pulled her down with me. There was no better therapy than sleep for things like that.

I waited as she got comfortable and dozed off before I let myself succumb to the alluring darkness.

When I woke up, Ruth was gone. I could tell that it was late morning by the way the light seeped through the thick curtains covering the windows.

I got to my feet and took a quick back and changed before leaving the room to find Ruth.

I went to check Dante's room and found the room half trashed but empty.

I checked Hazel's ward and found Ruth and Dante sitting beside Hazel's bed. They weren't saying anything, they were just staring at Hazel's immobile form with their eyes unfocused.

I opened the door and entered the room to find both of their gazes on me. "Did you sleep well?" Ruth asked in a whisper to not wake Hazel up.

Before I could answer, Hazel stirred on the bed and all of our gazes snapped to her.

She raised her head slightly before letting it fall back down. She blinked several times before recognizing our presence in the room.

Her eyes turned to Dante who looked at her with red, teary eyes, and I could see her blink back the tears forming in her eyes.

Neither Dante nor Ruth asked why she did it. I felt like an intruder, but I felt like I had to be there for Ruth.

No one dared to speak for the next few minutes, and it was Hazel who broke the silence. "I am going to Italy,"

Dante's jaw ticked with emotion, but he didn't say anything. Ruth bit her lip to control herself, but she didn't say anything either.

Dante rose and took a step towards Hazel's direction. She didn't make any move to stop him, nor did she complain. She didn't move as he bent a little and placed a kiss on her forehead and spoke, "Take care of yourself,"

Hazel nodded, and I could tell that she was trying very hard to keep herself from breaking down, especially when Dante turned around and left the ward without another word.

Ruth followed Dante, but I stayed back. I had no clue what to say or do, I had never been in a situation even slightly similar to that.

"I don't know why you did it, but I hope you find peace, Hazel, and I hope you manage to sort everything out,"

Hazel nodded, but didn't say anything. In her heart, I could tell that she was regretting it. It was evident on her face. She was a kind soul, and she hated herself for the trouble she'd put her loved ones through.

What bugged me, as I walked back to Ruth's room, was the fact that no one from her family had shown up. Ruth had told me the other day that they hadn't informed her family since Hazel would probably be against it, but there were no calls from her family, no messages to check in on her in general.

I was about to ask Ruth, but she already had so many problems piling up, that I stopped myself.

She was aggressively packing her bag when I entered the room. I didn't say anything. There was nothing that could make her feel better at the moment.

Instead, I reached out to help her finish her work faster, but before I could get to her, her phone rang. It was placed on the bed, and since I was closer, I picked it up and handed it to her, "It's Biance,"

Her brows rose as she received the call. "What happened?" she asked. Her eyes widened and she cursed under her breath.

Suspiciously, a notification came from my phone at the same time and I immediately opened the message from Jack.

Ryan's bail got approved.

Before I could grasp the news Ruth threw the phone against the wall and breathed out, "Leah's missing,"

Follow me on Instagram @janushi_raichura for book updates!

The third part of The Billionaire's Code is coming soon!

Stay tuned for more updates—don't let your curiosity get hacked!